DISNEY

ENCANTO

A Tale of Three Sisters

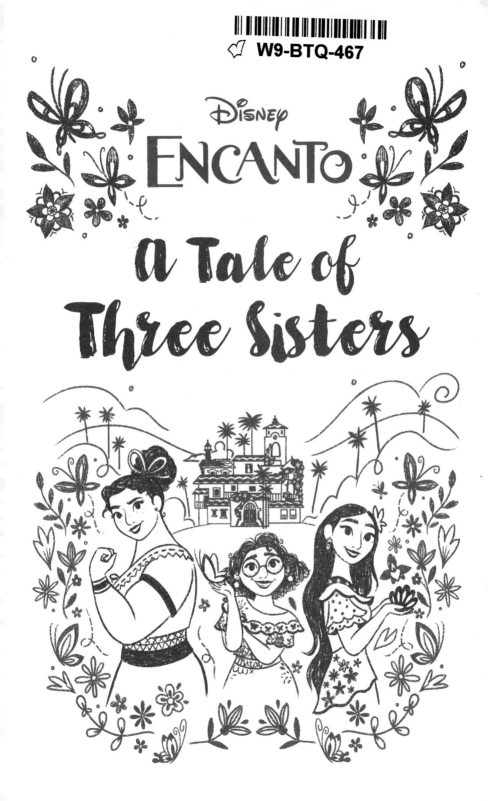

Copyright © 2022 Disney Enterprises, Inc. All rights reserved.

Illustrations by Paola Escobar © Disney Enterprises, Inc.
Design by Winnie Ho
Composition and layout by Susan Gerber

Published by Disney Press, an imprint of Buena Vista Books, Inc.
No part of this book may be reproduced or transmitted in any form
or by any means, electronic or mechanical, including photocopying,
recording, or by any information storage and retrieval system, without
written permission from the publisher. For information address
Disney Press, 1200 Grand Central Avenue, Glendale, California 91201.

First Paperback Edition, February 2022
10 9 8 7 6 5 4 3 2 1
FAC-025438-22035

Printed in the United States of America
This book is set in Weiss Std.

Library of Congress Control Number: 2021932126
ISBN 978-1-368-09218-0

Visit disneybooks.com

SUSTAINABLE
FORESTRY
INITIATIVE

Certified Sourcing

www.sfiprogram.org
SFI-01054

The SFI label applies to the text stock

DISNEY
ENCANTO

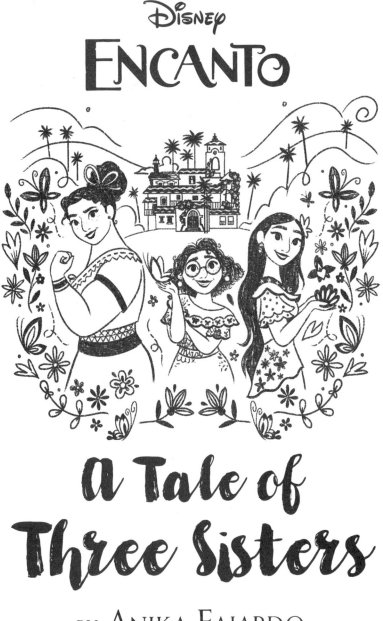

A Tale of
Three Sisters

BY ANIKA FAJARDO

 PRESS

Los Angeles • New York

Familia

ALMA

AGUSTÍN

JULIETA

ISABELA

LUISA

MIRABEL

Madrigal

PEDRO

BRUNO

PEPA

FELIX

DOLORES

CAMILO

ANTONIO

Prologue

ONCE UPON A TIME there was a family. Pedro and Alma Madrigal, the proud parents of triplets, loved their babies deeply, as parents do. And so, in order to protect and care for their little ones, they set out to find a new home and create a better life.

With only the glow of a single candle to light the way, the parents and their three babies—two girls and a boy—led others who, like them, were seeking a place of peace and safety. They traveled over difficult and treacherous terrain. They faced steep cliffs and narrow paths, harsh weather, and threatening bandits. Pedro and Alma had promised to make a new life, and they didn't—*wouldn't*—give up.

But the journey's dangers were many. From the banks of a swift-moving river, the travelers struggled to cross the rushing water. Step by treacherous step, they made their way through it. Holding her babies tightly, Alma Madrigal hesitated. The water was fast, and in places, deep. But the look of encouragement in Pedro's eyes convinced her that everything would be okay.

She was exhausted by the time she reached the other shore. And she refused to let go of her husband's hand. Then bandits appeared and threatened the travelers. As they approached, Pedro braved the enemies so his family could survive.

When Pedro died, Alma was heartbroken. But she knew she had to protect her children. Huddled with her babies, Alma watched the candle flicker and dim. The danger was approaching again. But just as the light was about to be extinguished, she found a miracle. Before her eyes, the little candle filled with magic. It burned brightly, drawing butterflies to itself, and banished the darkness. It fought off the bandits. The candle became an eternal flame and created a place of wonder.

An Encanto.

Their new home was nestled between tall mountains. The steep slopes protected a lush and vibrant valley. Waterfalls sparkled. Palm trees swayed. Flowers bloomed. And in the center of the Encanto, a fantastical house sprouted from the earth. The house itself came to life and filled with magic.

Alma was the heart of the Encanto. Her three children, each of whom was also imbued with a magical gift, sustained her.

As the years passed, the family thrived. The triplets married and had children of their own.

The house changed and expanded, always making room for each new family member. A flourishing town grew. The Encanto became a paradise for all who lived there, and the Madrigals were at the center of it.

Chapter 1 * Mirabel

EVERYTHING IS BLURRY, but I don't need my glasses to know that I'm waking up in the nursery that I share with my little cousin, Antonio. I squint against the bright sun shining directly on my face. *Ugh!* Teenagers shouldn't be woken up this early. Stretching and rubbing the sleep out of my eyes, I yawn—and then I remember what today is. I sit up and shove my glasses on my face.

Today is Antonio's fifth birthday! And more important, it's his gift day. Tonight, if all goes well, he'll be sleeping in his new room. His own room. I wonder what his gift will be. Now with clear vision, I look across the room to Antonio's bed. But instead of finding a little brown-haired boy, all I see is his bare mattress. Where *is* my primito?

I scramble out of bed. The drawers of my dresser fly open and I wiggle out of my nightgown and into my skirt and blouse—ignoring the stitching coming loose on the butterfly I embroidered last night. Never mind. I'll fix that later. What's important is finding Antonio.

"Buenos días, Casita," I call to the house as I leave the nursery. Casita catches the door before it slams, closing it gently. "Sorry, Casita," I say to my house—my beloved magical house. I pat the railing and gaze down at the courtyard. "Has anyone seen Antonio?"

But no one is below. I fly down the stairs. I

almost trip, but Casita gently cradles me with the rug. "Gracias!"

Today everyone is going to be busy, and I really want to help. I head to the dining room. Where is Mamá? I might be only fifteen—the youngest of me and my two sisters—but I can still be useful. I get out the special Madrigal plates, a different one for each person, to set the table.

It's so stuffy in here. "Casita, open the shutters!" I request.

The house flings them open with a clatter, revealing my view of the world: the Encanto. The magical valley where we live is surrounded by steep mountains that rise into puffy clouds. The slopes are rocky and dotted with trees, coffee plants, and blooming flowers. The mountains are often fuzzy, partially obscured by low-hanging mist that swirls in the evening as the sun sets. From the upstairs windows in Casita, you can see the town with its cobbled streets, a church with a pretty steeple, and neat white buildings with red roof tiles. Each house in town has blooming window boxes and brightly painted shutters.

In the middle of the Encanto is our house. Casita. When you walk toward the house after a trip into town, you can see the bushy bougainvillea that climbs up the terra-cotta walls. A chimney usually puffs a stream of wood smoke from the kitchen. The tower at the back of the house stands over it all like a soldier keeping watch.

There's so much to do, but I lean out the window and take a deep breath. Mangos. Black soil. Plátanos. Orchids. Fluffy clouds. I can smell it all. The scent of home. I close my eyes, feeling like maybe everything is going to be all—

"When's the magic gift going to happen?" someone calls.

I open one eye. Below me, just under the kitchen window, I find niños from town peering into the house, ever curious, always pestering me.

They are fascinated by my family and our house. And they always want to hear a story. And I never mind telling them one. "Who's asking?"

"Us!"

A little face pops up. "Me!"

"All of us!"

I laugh. "The magic will happen at my cousin's ceremony tonight," I say, going back to setting the table. "And it's gotta be perfect."

"Why?"

"Because we are the Familia Madrigal."

"What's his gift gonna be?" one of the children asks.

"What's *your* gift?" another shouts.

I ignore that question. Instead, I carefully lay out my sisters' plates and my aunt's cup and my grandmother's silverware. "We're going to find out what Antonio's gift will be," I tell them.

"What's your part?" asks someone with a little voice.

What *is* my part? I hope my family will let me be part of Antonio's special day. I may be different, but I can still help.

I decide to stall. I tell the kids, "I can't just tell you my part. Because if you don't see the whole picture, you don't see anything at all."

The table is set, ready for breakfast. I hear the sounds of my family waking up, starting their days. There's a banging of pots and pans from the kitchen. Someone is singing in a deep baritone. Giggles snake downstairs, and the thud of heavy things dropping adds a syncopated beat to the calling of macaws. Soon my whole family will crowd into the dining room for breakfast, but I feel too excited to sit around waiting. It's Antonio's gift day, after all.

"Windows!" I cry, and Casita polishes the windows. "Floors!" The carpets are clean and the floors shine. "Doors!" I shout as I come into the courtyard. In the balcony above me, all the doors glow—well, all but two. I shake my head, trying to clean out the worries from my brain. See? I can't wait around. I like to be moving and doing. I call, "Let's go!"

The house flings open the front door and I'm greeted by the sunny morning. I almost trip over children gathered outside waiting for me. I sling my mochila over my shoulder and head down the road toward town.

"Where are you going?" The children pester me. "What are you doing?"

I turn and wave to Casita. The children watch wide-eyed as the house winks back at me using a shutter.

"Will you tell us about your family?" asks one of the little boys as my parents, uncle, aunt, and cousins peek out of windows, head into the yard, and do all the odd things they do each morning.

"Don't you know?" I ask, watching these people I know so well and love so much. Even when they're annoying—which seems to be more and more often.

 11

"Um," the boy says. I can see that I've embarrassed him. I didn't mean to, but I'm surprised these kids don't know all about the Madrigal family's gifts. The whole town knows everything about us.

"There's just so many," he says shyly, "I can't remember who's who."

"Will you tell us?"

I smile at the kids. I'm happy to explain my family to them, glad to be useful for something. The children follow me into town, where we see a line of people.

"Well, this is Mamá—you can call her Julieta." Mamá waves at me as she tends to the people in line waiting for her. "Her gift is healing with food. Whatever is wrong with you, she can fix with a meal. Or sometimes just a snack." I cut in the line—I'm her daughter, after all—and she gives me an arepa and an embarrassing kiss. "Where was I?" I ask with my mouth full.

"Your mom," one of the kids prompts.

"Right." And I tell the niños about my family. The magical family Madrigal.

But they seem confused at first. "Which one is—" begins one.

"It's not that hard to remember who's who," says a young woman, appearing out of nowhere.

The kids jump in surprise. "That's my cousin Dolores," I explain as she laughs.

"Don't forget," my older cousin says to the children, "I have super hearing. Whispers are like gritos to me."

"In other words," I say, "watch what you say around her." Dolores nods. "Actually, watch what you say anywhere. She can hear a pin drop."

"What was that?" Dolores says, listening to something none of us can hear. "Oh, my mom needs me. She's at the house." Even from town, we can see the Casa Madrigal. The sun casts a warm, dewy glow over the roof tiles.

"My tía, Pepa, is her mom," I explain as Dolores

rushes away. "Obviously, she's in a good mood today. After all, it's her youngest son's gift day. Her magic is controlling—or sometimes *not* controlling—the weather."

"So when it rains . . ." a little boy says.

"Yep," I say. "Pepa is probably having a bad day."

The boy giggles but stops as he sees a young woman carrying a wagon over her head, her muscles not even showing the strain.

"That's my sister Luisa," I say. Her gift is strength. "She must be helping get ready for Antonio's gift ceremony," I explain to the children, who watch her openmouthed.

Luisa brings the wagon to where Mamá is running her clinic. She sets it down gently. "Thank you, Luisa," calls my mother. Luisa smiles proudly and then scarfs down the arepas Mamá tosses her way.

"Oh, look," I say to the children. "Here comes my uncle Felix—" But then my uncle shifts into the form of a goofy teenage boy. We can't help laughing as my uncle suddenly becomes my giggling fifteen-year-old cousin. "That's Camilo. He's a troublemaker," I say. "Watch out for him—his gift is shape-shifting. You never know who he'll pop up as."

The children laugh once more as Camilo changes into one of them and then shifts back into his magical Madrigal self again. There's nothing he loves more than making people laugh.

"Ignore him," I say. "Come on!" The children follow me as we head to the town's busy plaza.

In the vibrant space, several stands are set up. Villagers sell fruits—mangos, maracuyas, bananas, chontaduros—from big baskets. Another stall sells loaves of pan, plates of buñuelos, and bags of pandebonos. A couple of women haggle over the price of a handwoven cloth. They argue with twinkles in their eyes—the negotiations are half the fun! At a café, a group of old men hold a heated discussion over cups of black coffee. They roll up their sleeves and ask the dueño for more coffee. On a bench in the shade of a jacaranda tree, an elderly couple sit side by side, watching a baby toddle toward them. The woman scoops up the grandbaby in her arms and plants a loud besito on his cheek.

A couple of the kids drift off to join a game of soccer happening in the middle of the plaza. I try on a wide-brimmed hat from the hat guy. I model the hat for the children, but they laugh at me. Guess I'm not buying a hat today. At a market stand selling helados, we find my dad and uncle, one tall and thin, one short and one—um—not thin.

"Hola!" shouts Papá.

"That's my dad, Agustín," I say, waving at my skinny papá, "and *that's* my Uncle Felix."

Felix doesn't look up. I don't know what those two find to talk about, but they're always discussing something.

A child tugs on my sleeve. "What's their magic?"

I shake my head. "They married into the Familia Madrigal. They don't have magical gifts. But they have each other," I add with a smile. The two men resume their conversation.

"Isn't there another uncle?" one of the kids asks.

I frown. "Well, my tío Bruno . . ." I don't know how to explain that I'm not sure what happened to Bruno. What I do know is that we don't talk about Bruno. "He disappeared," I say. "He's gone."

Luckily, the children are distracted by a tall, handsome man standing near my dad.

"How about him? Is he related to you?"

"No." I laugh. "But he'd like to be. He wants to marry my sister Isabela," I add in a whisper.

"Is she really as perfect as they say?" asks a little girl. "Where is she?"

"You can't miss her," I say, pointing to where the handsome Mariano is staring. My oldest sister, Isabela, is beautiful. No one can resist her charm. The sellers hand her free fruits and dulces, ask to smell the flowers in her hair. Her gift is a green thumb, although I don't know why they call it that. Nothing about her is green. Today she wears a lavender and cream dress with flowers that match perfectly. No loose threads on *her* clothes. Her hair is pulled up on one side and falls over her shoulders in gorgeous soft curls. Her face is beautiful, serene, and calm. It's really hard to get mad at her because she's just so nice. Except to me sometimes. But I am her little sister.

The little girl gazes at Isabela like she just saw an angel.

"Come on, niñita," I say, pulling the girl along. "Time to head back to la Casa."

We arrive back home, the children chattering behind me. I'm smiling and happy. Today is going to be amazing. And I won't worry—

Suddenly, a hush falls over the kids. I look up. There, in the doorway, is my grandmother.

"Buenos días," my abuela says.

"Who's that?" a child whispers.

"That's my grandmother, Abuela Alma," I whisper. "She's the head of the family." I hold up my finger to my lips to tell the kids to be quiet. We always have to be respectful and obedient around Abuela. I try, even though sometimes it's really hard.

"What are you doing, Mirabel?" Abuela strides toward me, the keys on her chatelaine jingling.

"Oh, um, they—" I look around, but the kids are hiding from view. "They were just asking about the family."

"She was about to tell us about her super awesome gift!" calls out one of the brave boys.

"Mirabel's gift?" Dolores, her ears pricked, appears out of nowhere. "What's Mirabel's gift?" she repeats. My cousin Dolores, who can hear music, whispers, or secrets from miles away, spends more time listening than talking, so I'm hoping she won't answer the children.

"Yeah, she was about to tell us about her super-awesome gift—"

"Mirabel's gift?" Luisa is loaded down with a wagon, which she carries as if it were as light as a feather pillow. "She didn't get one."

"W-wha—" stammer the children. I can't tell if they are gaping at my sister's Herculean strength or my lack of a gift.

I hold my head up high. "It's true. I don't have a gift." I fiddle with the embroidery on my skirt. Oh dear, another thread has come loose. I straighten. "But gift or no gift, I am just as special as the rest of my family."

I know I sound more confident than I feel.

Chapter 2 * Isabela

THE FLORAL ARCHWAYS in the courtyard of Casita must be just right for Antonio's gift ceremony tonight. Abuela Alma said everything has to be perfect. I think I'll put one archway here and one more at the foot of the staircase. I'm wondering if the flowers should be color coordinated or match exactly, when Papá stumbles by.

"Are you okay, Papi?" I ask. He's covered in

ugly welts—puffy red blotches cover his face, and his hands are blown up like big balloons. I wonder if Mamá has seen this.

"Bee stings." He shrugs.

"You'd better go see Mamá," I say. He looks like he's in pain, and I wish my gift were a bit more useful, like my mom's. Flowers can't cure bee stings. In fact, sometimes they cause them.

"Oh, Agustín, mi amor!" Mamá cries. "¿Qué pasó?" She sees my dad and gets to work curing him. "Where's Mirabel?" she asks as she pulls a couple arepas from her apron pocket.

"I think she's working on decorations," Papá mumbles through his arepa. "She's trying so hard. I know just how she feels. When me and Felix married into this family, we were outsiders—no gifts. Everyone else was so exceptional. Ouch!" he exclaims as Mamá examines a particularly gruesome-looking sting. "It was easy to feel, um, 'un-ceptional' sometimes."

"Thanks, Papi." I look up and find Mirabel

standing near our dad. Her arms are loaded down with supplies. Of some kind. She's always got a plan. Of some kind.

"I'm just saying, Mira," he says to her. He rubs his face; the welts are gone. "I get it."

"If you need to talk, corazón . . ." Mamá says.

Oh, Mamá, I think, *you'll never get her to talk about it.*

Sure enough, Mirabel snaps, "I'm fine!"

They're just trying to help, I want to scold her. But I say nothing. After all, if you can't say something nice, don't say anything at all. Something I tend to forget when talking to my littlest sister.

"You have nothing to prove," both my parents say in unison as they head back to the house with Mirabel.

The moment they're gone, I hear someone call out.

"Perdón?"

I look up from my hydrangeas and roses to see the donkey delivery guy coming up the path.

"Excuse me?" he calls out again.

 23

I wipe my hands on my apron. Deliveries at the Casa Madrigal are often for me. This might be a present from Mariano Guzmán. Everyone expects us to get married—someday. He's sent me things before like chocolates or little trinkets. Sometimes he sends me bouquets of flowers, even though I have plenty of those.

But instead of handing me a package, the delivery guy says, "I'm looking for Mirabel."

I'm relieved, actually. I don't need any more flowers. And it'll be nice for Mirabel to get something, especially today

"This is her special delivery," the donkey man says. "Err . . . her *not*-special special delivery. Since she's the one with no gift. Ha, ha."

Poor Mirabel. Sometimes I wonder what it would be like not to have a gift. And sometimes I wonder if it might be kind of nice.

"Here she comes," I say.

Mirabel is just opening the front door.

 24

"Hey, Mirabel," the delivery guy says, "tell Antonio good luck tonight." He hands over a bundle of paper, silk, ribbon, and thread. "If he gets a gift," the guy continues, "it means that last ceremony was just the disappointing exception."

Mirabel nods. I think I might see an eye roll.

"Last one being yours," the delivery guy adds. "That did not work." As if she needs clarification about the most disappointing moment of her life.

The guy leads his donkey away, and she heads back into the house. I shake my head. Sadly, I know that things don't always turn out . . . quite right for my sister. I would go over and ask her if I can help, but there's no point. She probably wouldn't accept my assistance even if I offered it. She always wants stuff done her own way. I turn back to my archway and adjust a couple of blossoms. A rose's thorn snags my finger. It doesn't really hurt, but it leaves a pinprick of blood. I shake away the sting. As I move my hand, more blossoms sprout on the branch. I stand back. Almost perfect. Okay, they *are* perfect.

As I prepare to go inside, I hear someone say, "I can't believe Mirabel doesn't have a gift."

The village children are wandering back to town. Two are skipping, one is collecting pebbles, and one is walking backward.

"I would be sad if I were her," one of the little girls says.

I would be sad, too. I've never said anything to Mirabel, but her gift day was one of the saddest days of my life. I remember when Mamá walked with her down the aisle. Little five-year-old Mirabel wore a necklace of daisies that I had made her. She was such a cute kid—that was when her wild hair looked adorable instead of just messy. I remember how her eyes shone with excitement on her fifth birthday as she walked toward her glowing door—her destiny.

Mirabel appears, carrying not only her supplies from earlier but also all the junk the delivery guy delivered. "Well, my little friend," she says to the girl, "I am not sad, because the truth is, gift or no gift, I am just as special as the rest of my family."

The kids exchange glances with one another and then with me.

"Maybe your gift is being in denial," one of the children says.

They run off laughing and I hide my giggle with a flower while Mirabel turns bright red. She stomps into the house, struggling under the weight of her bundles. She should get Luisa to help her with that.

When I finish with the flowers outside, I head inside, where it seems like everyone is yelling instructions to Luisa.

"Luisa! We need the piano up here!"

"Lift it a little higher!"

"Camilo," Abuela calls, "we need another José."

My cousin, always ready to help, shape-shifts into the tall José from town and is instantly big enough to hang the banner above Antonio's new door. ANTONIO!! it says. I don't tell them it's a little crooked.

"My baby's night has to be perfect," Pepa says, worried. "And if it's not perfect . . ."

She paces and the wind in the courtyard picks up.

"Amor," Felix says, "you're tornadoing the flowers."

"Flowers?" I say. I survey the courtyard where the ceremony will be held. One more floral archway should be good. Maybe I'll add flowers to the staircase, too. I look up at the railing that runs around the courtyard, protecting the balcony where all the family doors are, and decorate it with more flowers.

I stand back and admire my work. "Please, don't clap," I say as Dolores gushes.

Mirabel is at my side. In surprise, I unintentionally shoot a puff of petals in her direction. A total accident, I swear. To cover up my mistake, I snap at her, "Relax, no one's looking at you."

"They're looking at you because . . . you're pretty, um . . ." She pauses. "Well, you are pretty. Obviously. Gah!" She sulks away.

My sister is so irritating sometimes.

A little later, I hear a *snip, snip* of scissors. Craning my neck, I can see that Mirabel has set up her crafting on the balcony in front of what will become Antonio's door—we hope. The supplies from the donkey delivery guy are scattered around her.

"What are you doing, Mirabel?"

Abuela's stern voice disrupts the quiet of the courtyard. I'm not sure where she came from, but she is standing over Mirabel, watching her do her project. That would make me so nervous.

"Making decorations. For Antonio. I actually made this for you. . . ." Mirabel holds up her creation. I'm not sure what it is and, clearly, neither does Abuela. It's got colored paper and candles and—oh, dear—now it's on fire.

"Perhaps you should leave the decorations to

someone else?" Abuela says as Mirabel stamps out the flames.

Casita helps clean the mess, but the scent of smoke hangs in the air. Abuela descends the stairs and glances at the sky above the courtyard. The brilliant blue is interrupted by a darkening cloud. "Pepa!" Abuela calls.

My aunt bustles out from the kitchen.

"Pepa, the sky has a cloud."

"I know, Mamá, but . . ." She throws up her hands. Pepa's worries have gathered into a storm cloud. She blinks away the raindrops falling in her eyes.

"Oh, Pepa," says Abuela, looking at her daughter. "Maybe try to control your feelings a little."

"But I can't find Antonio anywhere!"

"I bet I can find him!" Mirabel offers. She jumps up. Antonio is never far from her. He adores my sister, which is good. Having someone who looks up to her seems to make the no-gift thing more bearable. I wonder how it will be when (if?) Antonio gets his.

"No, Mirabel," Abuela says, "I'm sure you need to get, uh, cleaned up." She looks Mirabel up and down. Her dress has a few loose threads and now there's a black smudge on her skirt from the craft-induced-fire incident.

"It's no problem. Anything I can do to help."

My heart hurts for Mirabel; she wants to help so much, but it usually goes, well, badly. I hope Antonio has a wonderful, perfect gift day—like mine. I was the first granddaughter, and Abuela couldn't wait to find out my power. She was so proud when flowers and vines grew around my door. I remember walking into my pink room with my grandmother and my parents. They oohed and aahed at the beauty of plants and nature. My room was—is—amazing, and my gift is everything to me.

"I know you want to help, Nieta," Abuela says to

her. "But tonight must go perfectly. Do you under-stand?" Mirabel nods. "The whole town relies on our family, on our gifts. So maybe the best way for you to help is to . . ." She pauses. "Maybe the best way for you to help is to step aside, let the rest of the family do what they do best, okay?"

Mirabel looks like she just lost her favorite thing in the whole world. She attempts a smile, but she doesn't fool me. "Yeah, no problem." She trudges toward her room.

"Pepa, amor," Abuela calls, her attention already elsewhere, "the wind!"

"Mamá," I hear. Now that Mirabel is out of sight, my own mother appears from the kitchen, wiping her hands on her apron. "Be nice to Mirabel, okay? You know tonight will be hard for her."

"Julieta, if this gift ceremony doesn't go well," Abuela says, "tonight will be hard for all of us."

I think back again to Mirabel's ceremony ten years ago. We were so excited. And then—nothing. When she went to open her door—the door to what was supposed to be her new room—nothing happened. When she touched the doorknob, the magic faded. Abuela turned away.

My cousin Dolores told me she heard little Mirabel crying that night back in the nursery. I can't even imagine what it would be like to not have my own room. To be stuck in the nursery. Will she be there forever?

Chapter 3 * Mirabel

BEFORE I OPEN the nursery door, Abuela's voice drifts up from the courtyard. "Tonight will be hard for us all," she says.

She's right. I slam the door shut and flop on my bed. I stare up at the ceiling, which I've decorated with drawings of Pepa's rainbows, Isabela's flowers, Luisa's boulders, and bowls of Mamá's arroz con pollo.

I flip over. Abuela's voice echoes in my head. *The best way for you to help is to step aside.* Across the room, Antonio's clothes are packed in a suitcase and a couple wooden crates, ready to move to his new room. A move I'll never make. I realize that I'm the last Madrigal to be in the unmagical nursery. Stuck here forever. Alone. I spot one of Antonio's little shoes peeking out from the crate. I'm going to miss his cute snores and his morning giggles. Where is he, anyway?

I hear a scritch-scratch under the bed and smile. I *knew* I could find him.

"Drawer," I say. "Package."

My room may not be magical like everyone else's, but my beloved Casita bumps my dresser drawer with a wallboard and it flies open, catapulting a wrapped package into my hands.

"Gracias."

Scritch-scritch, I hear again. *Shuffle, shuffle.* The sound is coming from under the bed. I loop my fingers in the ribbons of the present and let it dangle over the edge.

"Everyone's looking for you." I wiggle the present in my fingers. I remember how much I loved presents when I was little. "This present will self-destruct if you don't take it in three, two, one—"

A little hand pops out from under the bed. Both it and the present disappear. I laugh and squeeze under the bed, too, curling up with my primito. "There you are. Are you nervous?"

He shrugs. His eyes don't leave my present in his hands.

"You have nothing to worry about."

He nods again, still staring at the present.

The last thing he needs to be concerned about is that he'll end up like me—with no magical gift. He's so young, I just want him to enjoy his special day. "You're going to get your gift," I reassure him, "and open your door. And it's going to be the coolest thing ever. I know it."

Antonio mumbles something.

"What?" He's very shy, often quiet. Sometimes my aunt worries about him (and causes all sorts of trouble with the weather). But I figure we all grow at different rates. We all find our voices on our own schedule.

"What if it doesn't work?" he repeats.

"Well, in that impossible scenario, then you'll stay here in the nursery. Forever. With me. I'd get you all to myself." I squeeze his small brown hand.

"I wish you could have a door," Antonio whispers.

"You don't have to worry about me. I have an amazing family, an amazing house, and an amazing you." I don't want Antonio to be sad or scared. But mostly, I don't want what happened to me to happen to him. I say brightly, "Seeing you get your special gift, your door, is going to make me way more happy than anything." A grin slowly spreads across his face. "But, alas, I'm going to miss having the world's best roomie."

I nod toward the wrapped present clutched in his hand. Antonio tears into the paper. When he opens the box and finds the little stuffed jaguar I knitted, he hugs it tightly. The jaguar is a little lumpy and the stitching is uneven, but as I watch him squeezing it, I know it doesn't have to be perfect. Just perfect for Antonio.

"I know you're an animal guy. And I made this for you so when you move into your cool new room, you always have something to snuggle with."

Antonio squeezes the jaguar again. I feel my own heart squeeze with happiness for my cousin. "Are you ready, hombrecito?"

He nods shyly.

Casita's floorboards rattle, kicking us out. I roll out from under the bed and push my glasses up on my nose. Antonio rolls out behind me. "But first, one more squeeze," I say.

I squeeze Antonio, and Antonio squeezes the jaguar. We're ready.

I hope.

 39

Chapter 4 * Luisa

I SWIPE A DRIP OF SWEAT from my brow. Hopefully Abuela doesn't notice. I'm not supposed to get tired or worn out. She asked me to set up the fireworks in back of the house in preparation for Antonio's big day, but first I had to clear away some brush and dead leaves—fire hazard, you know. And while I was cleaning that up, I noticed that a couple of trees needed their branches trimmed, so

I did that. And then Abuela wanted me to move the piano—first to the courtyard, then upstairs. I still have to move the benches and tables for the guests, but I've been parking the townspeople's donkeys and carts all afternoon. Who knew this many people were interested in another gift day at the Madrigals' place? Well, I suppose since the last one didn't go so well . . .

"Luisa!" Tía Pepa calls. She's being followed by a shiny rainbow—proof of how pleased she is that it's finally Antonio's gift day. I wave. I'm about to congratulate her, and I hold out my arms for a hug (everyone loves my hugs because I'm so strong). Instead, my tía says, "Could you move these benches?"

"Sí," I answer, straightening my bun and pulling it tight. Guess I'm not getting a hug right now. I stack the benches like firewood and carry them through to the courtyard. On my way back out-side, I hear Felix.

"Luisa!"

"What do you need?" I ask in my helpful tone. He's grinning broadly. Maybe *he* wants to hug me?

"It's time to—vámonos!" And suddenly it's not Felix at all, but Camilo shape-shifting from his father back to himself.

I roll my eyes. He doesn't seem to understand that we need to make sure everything is done by the time the ceremony begins. "Camilo," I grumble, "I don't have time for your games. I have work to do."

Camilo just giggles himself into Antonio and then back into himself as he races away, likely to play a trick on another family member.

While my cousin was distracting me, several more carts and donkeys arrived. I sigh. I'm happy to help; I mean, I *want* to help. I love helping. Just need a moment to catch my breath. I place a number on each donkey before I pick them up and park them side by side over by the others.

"Hija!" my mother calls. I spin around and almost trip. What does she want now? It's so hard to keep track of everything. "Come into the court-yard, Luisa. It's time to begin."

Oh, she doesn't need my strength—right now. "¡Ya vengo!" I call. I can't believe it's already time to begin Antonio's ceremony. The day flies by when you're busy . . . like me. "I'm coming, Mamá."

I head toward the courtyard and pass Felix—the real Felix. "Papito," he says to Antonio, who looks a little nervous. I don't blame him. "There you are. Ready for the big show?"

Pepa hugs her boy. "Look at you, all grown up." She can't help starting to cry. And when she cries, so does the sky.

"Amor," Felix says gently, "you're raining on his outfit."

Another Felix says, "You make-a your papa proud—"

"I don't sound like that," the real Felix protests.

The other Felix—obviously Camilo, not fool-ing anyone—mimics, "I don't sounds like that."

"Abuela says it's time," Dolores says.

I run over to stand between Mamá and Papá. Isabela is on the other side of Papá. I look around. Where's Mirabel? I wonder if she's feeling kind of lousy right now.

"Fifty years ago," Abuela Alma begins. She is standing at the top of the stairs near Antonio's door. The ANTONIO!! banner sags a bit, but the door glows.

The crowd hushes. The courtyard is filled with members of the Madrigal family and also guests from town. Many of them were here ten years ago for Mirabel's gift day. My palms are clammy. I'm so nervous for Antonio and Abuela and Mirabel. For everyone.

Abuela holds the family's magic candle. The sun is just disappearing behind the mountains surrounding the Encanto. The candle's flame throws warm shadows on the walls of the courtyard. I can feel Casita smiling with pride. Heck, *I'm* smiling with pride. I cross my fingers. I hope everything turns out okay.

"Fifty years ago, on the night of my Pedro's great sacrifice, this candle blessed us with a miracle." The candle glows more brightly in Abuela's hands. "And the greatest honor of our family has been to use our blessings to serve this beloved community. Tonight, we come together once more as another steps into the light. To make us proud."

Casita spotlights Antonio, trying to nudge him out from behind a shadow at one end of the courtyard. The guests crane their necks, attempting to get a good look at our littlest Madrigal. He seems so small, so young. His eyes are big with uncertainty. I remember feeling like that on my gift day. It's scary to have everyone watching you. I remember how alone I felt. My big sister, Isabela, had made me a crown of flowers, and that helped me feel brave, knowing she was there for me. Because I'm so strong, no one ever thinks about whether I ever feel scared or overwhelmed. But, to tell the truth, I do sometimes.

"Tonight," Abuela continues, "we come together

once more as another earns our miracle and steps into the light."

"I need you," we hear Antonio whisper.

Who is he talking to? Me? I'm often needed. To lift something heavy, maybe to move a tree or the general store. The usual stuff. I begin to rise. But Mamá holds out her hand to stop me.

"I can't." I hear Mirabel's voice.

The people whisper, wondering where the voice is coming from. Then we spot her hidden behind a pillar. Antonio's eyes fill. He begins to tremble. And then Mirabel steps out from the shadow. She takes his little hand and leads him forward. She's holding her head high. Physically I am strong, but I don't think I could ever be that strong. I would be a blubbering mess.

"Let's get you to your door," Mirabel says firmly. She doesn't look worried at all. I'm relieved no one needs me right now.

We watch as Mirabel leads Antonio across the courtyard. Hand in hand, they march up the stairs to the balcony that spans the second floor. We strain to see as the pair passes the family portraits that line the walls, photos of each family member's gift day. The day Dolores got her gift of hearing. The smile on Mamá's face when she was five years old and got the gift of healing. The goofy grin of Camilo, the sweet smile of Pepa. The image of Abuelo Pedro.

Antonio grips Mirabel's hand more firmly as they pass the doors to each person's room. The plain nursery door, my door embedded with weights and dumbbells, Isabela's floral door that we can smell from all the way down here. They pass a stairway that leads to a door covered in cobwebs—no one talks about that. And, at last, they stand in front of Antonio's door, which glows brighter as he nears. My aunt cries out. She must be so nervous. I glance at her and see that a miniature tornado is threatening to form above her head. What if Antonio doesn't get a gift, just like Mirabel didn't?

"Go on," Mirabel says, gently pushing him toward Abuela, who is waiting for him. I'm glad I'm not the one helping our primito. I would be shaking if I were Mirabel right now.

"Will you use your gift to serve this community?" Abuela solemnly asks Antonio. He nods, his eyes wide. "Will you earn the miracle and make us proud?" He nods again. Abuela sweeps her arm in a grand gesture toward his glowing door.

Antonio reaches out his hand. Then he snatches it back. Everyone inhales and holds their breath, both my family and everyone from town. Quickly, before he can change his mind, Antonio reaches toward the doorknob. Abuela's brow wrinkles with worry, strain, stress. I can tell she's reliving Mirabel's gift day.

But as Antonio grabs the knob, magic fills the balcony, the courtyard, the entire Casa. The glow of the door brightens. A toucan lands on Antonio's arm and croaks, nodding its head up and down excitedly.

"Yes!" says Antonio, his voice the loudest I've ever heard it. And the most confident. "I can understand you!"

Antonio's gift is communicating with animals! The crowd lets out its breath in one happy sigh. Cheers erupt. Tía Pepa is so excited, a hot wind starts blowing Isabela's flower petals everywhere. I whoop and holler. "Yes!" I shout. A python slithers toward Antonio as he slowly pushes his door open. In swoops a pair of colorful macaws that perch on the railing. A stripy-tailed coati scurries around in excitement, waiting for its turn to enter Antonio's room. A jaguar, its spots dark and its coat bright, bounds up the stairs toward my cousin, who gives it a huge bear hug—err, I mean, jaguar hug? I wonder if its hugs are better than mine.

Animals are everywhere, attracted to Antonio like moths to a flame. He laughs and hugs each one. Fireworks erupt over the house, and light from the explosions illuminates Abuela's face. I don't think

I've ever seen my grandmother so relieved in my life. Except maybe that time I lifted three fallen wax palms off her brand-new carriage.

"We have a new gift!" she proclaims.

Chapter 5 * Mirabel

I DAWDLE BEHIND THE OTHERS as they follow Antonio into his room. I'm happy for him—I really am. Shy Antonio is the greeter, all smiles and handshakes as the Familia Madrigal and the townspeople pour in. Each time his door opens, the sound of raucous laughter—both human and animal—escapes.

Now the sound of Abuela's jingling chatelaine

punctuates the party noises. "I knew you could do it." She's looking down at Antonio, her eyes full of pride. It's a look I've never seen directed at me. Watching Abuela embrace Antonio feels like when I have a scab on my knee; it's not that painful unless I pick at it. Abuela envelopes him into a tight, sheltering hug. "A gift just as special as you."

I think back to my gift day. Before the ceremony, Abuela came into my room and snuggled with me. She calmed my nerves much like I comforted Antonio this morning. She had just told me the story of the Madrigal candle, the one that created the Encanto and Casita. The one that blessed all of Abuela's children and grandchildren.

Together, cuddled close, we watched the flame. "Tonight, this candle will give you your gift, mi vida. Make your Abuelo's sacrifice matter. Earn our miracle. Make your family proud."

I remember being filled with pride and wonder at the thought of being graceful like my big sister Isabela or strong like my older sister Luisa or helpful like Mamá. "What do you think my gift will be, Abuelita?" I asked. I could see so many possibilities then.

"You are a wonder, Mirabel," Abuela said to me, her face full of love. "Whatever gift awaits will be just as special as you." I also remember the look of disappointment on my grandmother's face when I didn't get a gift. It was the last time she embraced me like that.

Antonio wiggles out of Abuela's grasp. He's too excited for long hugs. He takes her hand to pull her into his room. When I enter a few paces behind them, I gasp at what I see.

There are trees everywhere. Palo santo, wax palms. Animals jump from branch to branch. Quiet, shy Antonio leaps into the middle of them all. He bounds from a family of coatis to a pile of snakes. He swivels around the limbs of a humongous ceiba, slapping high fives with a bunch of tamarin monkeys.

"You wanna go where?" he says to the jaguar,

and hops on its back. "Whoooooaaaa!" Antonio yells as the animal tosses him in the air. It's as if he's suddenly who he was meant to be, I think as I watch him dunk his head under a waterfall. The kid who never liked a bath shakes off his wet hair with a chuckle. He jumps from rock to rock, crossing a sparkling stream where I think I see the pink back of a river dolphin. This must be what a Madrigal gift does: makes the person more themselves. Antonio's magical room is as unique and friendly as he is—and a big change from our little nursery.

"We need a picture, everyone!" Abuela calls. She waves over the family. "Come, come, come. It's a great night."

Isabela helps gather my tía and tío, my cousins. Lanterns light the way, and Tía Pepa is radiant with a full rainbow. Luisa carries a few logs to make a seating area. Mamá is handing out sweet obleas y arequipe to the guests. Felix and Dolores are working on some kind of music on the tiple, and

Camilo makes everyone laugh as he shifts between being one of the village kids and an obnoxious teenager—in other words, himself. Abuela beams at my sister as she lines up the familia. "It's a perfect night."

I push my glasses up on my nose. The Madrigals do look perfect. They're each unique and special. Each of them with a gift. I watch Abuela smile at her daughters and her grandchildren. Why doesn't she smile at me like that? I look around. There must be something I can do to make Abuela proud.

"¡Vengan!" someone shouts, rousing me from those painful memories. I blink away a tear. (I must be allergic to something in this jungle!) I need to try to be in this family. I need to find a way to earn my spot as a Madrigal. I smooth out my skirt and pat my hair. And then I step forward. I guess I'll just stand right—

"Everyone say 'Familia Madrigal'!"

The flashbulb bursts, a smile on every face. Except mine. Because I was one step away.

I've got to get away from Antonio's party before something I do or say ruins everything. The best way I can help my family now is clearly by not doing anything. They don't want me there. They don't need me. I watch Antonio ride the jaguar like a cowboy and smile sadly. Even Antonio is fine without me. He probably won't even need to cuddle with the stuffed toy I made him—now that he has the real thing. I slip out of the jungle room and into the quiet hallway. As Antonio's door shuts behind me, the sounds of the fiesta suddenly extinguish, like a candle being blown out.

I escape to my favorite spot—the roof. If I swing my leg up on the balcony over here and then grab onto the downspout there, I can hop to the flat area above the courtyard. From here I can see everything, and, even better, no one can see me. The tiles are still warm from the day's sun. I take off my shoes and soak in the heat. I look out over the Encanto. The trees are dark shadows, and Isabela's flowers that climb the walls glow. Across the courtyard, I see Abuela's room. She's at Antonio's party, but the Madrigal candle burns brightly in her window, just like it always does. The candle never melts, never drips, never goes out.

"The candle holds the miracle given to our family," Abuela told me on my fifth birthday, on the day I was supposed to get my gift. I asked her why we were given a miracle. "Love, sacrifice, a promise your abuelo made the night our children were born into a troubled world. He promised that we would find a new home, that our children would have a better life." I remember the tear in Abuela's eye as she told me this. "And when he was lost, the earth decided his promise would be kept." Even now I can feel the warmth of her hand as she touched my face. "The candle filled with magic, became an eternal flame."

Seeing the candle burn in Abuela's window

now is both comforting and a reminder of my lack of a gift.

Crack!

I startle at the sound. That did not sound right. When I look around, though, I see the toucan. It nods its head and croaks. Okay, maybe nothing's wrong except the usual I-didn't-get-a-gift-and-everyone-else-did stuff.

"Audience of one," I say aloud. The toucan makes a laughing noise. "That's a start." I get up and scramble to go back inside.

Clonk!

I pause as a roof title breaks free and tumbles into the courtyard below. That is definitely not right. I hurry down to the courtyard. The party in Antonio's room is still going strong. It's kind of a mess down here. The evidence of the ceremony is lying around: the flowers, the crooked benches. And then I see the fallen tile. It's broken in two pieces, and I pick one up.

"Ouch!" I exclaim as I cut my hand on its sharp

edge. "Casita?" I say, looking all around. "Are you okay?" I reach out and pat Casita's interior wall. The house usually likes when I do that.

But Casita shows no sign of appreciating the gesture. Instead, a small crack appears beneath my hand. I jerk it away. "Casita?" Okay, now I know for sure something isn't right.

Crunch!

The crack spreads. Another roof tile falls and smashes on the courtyard's brick floor. Now there are several cracks, each one spreading. They move along the wall and toward the stairway.

Crink!

Dozens of cracks race up the stairs toward the corridor of the family's doors. I run after them. Something is terribly wrong, I know it. I'm so worried about Casita. About the family. I just want them to be happy and safe. These cracks do not look like the way to being either safe or happy. The cracks continue past Isabela's door, the flowers faltering for a moment. I keep running. The cobwebs on the door no one talks about shiver as the cracks pass by. Ahead of me is Abuela's room and the candle in her window. The cracks seem to multiply in a hurry to get to her door. As I get nearer, though, the candle appears to dim. I stop and rub my eyes. I must be seeing things. I open them again. It *is* dimming. A glop of wax drips down the normally dripless candle. The magic Madrigal candle is definitely fading.

Chapter 6 * Isabela

ANTONIO'S ROOM IS LOVELY. It reminds me a little of my own, although not as colorful. And, of course, with many more animals. Where I have flowers, he has trees. Where I have neat rows of roses, he has tangled vines. Where the light in my room glows purple from the thousands of orchids, the light in here is yellow with lanterns and tinged with the green of so many plants. A gentle breeze always keeps my room the perfect temperature, but here there are gusts of wind and moments of warm stillness. The movement in Antonio's room is from the animals swinging, galloping, pouncing, and crawling. I glance over at my cousin. He couldn't be happier. He hops on a jaguar and together they race around the forest room, leaping over obstacles of lined-up chigüiros and splashing through sparkling brooks. He whoops with joy.

I know just how he feels. I remember how thrilled I was when I first saw my special room. I have loved flowers for as long as I can remember, and being surrounded by them was so thrilling. I remember spinning with joy, the skirt of my pretty white dress twirling and my grandmother and mother smiling at me. Your gift day is the most magical—and *important*—moment in your life as a Madrigal. It's what makes you a Madrigal.

Unless, of course, you're Mirabel. Then . . . well, then you're still a Madrigal, I suppose, but different.

"Isabela!" Mamá calls to me. I go to her right away; I don't like to make people wait. She holds out an oblea dripping with caramelly arequipe.

"No, gracias," I say, pushing away her food as politely as possible. "I wouldn't want to get that sticky mess on my dress."

Mamá takes a big bite. "Of course not, mija," she says with her mouth full. "I just wanted to tell you that Mariano was asking about you." She winks.

I can't help myself; I blush at the sound of his name.

"He's going to ask to marry you, Isabela."

"I know, Mamá." I brush a tendril of hair from my face. As I do, Mamá grabs my hand.

"What happened?" she asks, spotting the place where the rose thorn pricked me.

"It's nothing," I say. "Just a thorn. It doesn't hurt at all."

But Mamá can't help herself. "Here, eat this arepa. You won't spill a crumb." I obey and pop the corn cake in my mouth. It *is* delicious. My tiny injury disappears, and Mamá smiles, saying, "I'm so proud of you—"

"THE HOUSE IS IN DANGER!"

We both whip around to see Mirabel barreling through Antonio's door, her face white, her skirt dirty.

"THE HOUSE IS IN DANGER!"

Mirabel skids to a stop in front of us, panting.

"The candle . . . the wall . . ." she breathes. "The tiles were falling and there were cracks everywhere. And the candle almost went out."

Mamá gasps, her hand covering her face. Murmurs of alarm weave their way through the party guests.

Abuela marches toward Mirabel. She holds her head high. I know that look. It's the same thing I do when I walk through town, when I want everyone to trust me completely and think well of me.

Abuela's voice is low. "Show me."

Why, oh, why can't Mirabel behave? She's going to be in trouble.

With Mirabel and Abuela leading the way, we all proceed out of Antonio's room and into the courtyard.

And none of us sees anything.

I'm so embarrassed for Mirabel. Sure, a few of the flowers have dropped their petals. And one of the benches is tipped over. But otherwise, everything looks fine. What was she thinking? Mamá looks horrified and embarrassed. She runs her hand along the smooth wall of Casita.

"What . . . ? Casita?" Mirabel's mouth hangs open in a very unattractive way. "It started right there. The house was breaking. The candle was in trouble." Mirabel's eyes are pleading as she looks at Abuela.

Abuela sighs.

"Abuela, I promise. I—"

"That's enough." Abuela's voice is low and stern.

She's never, ever spoken to me like that. I would be so humiliated if I were Mirabel.

"But . . ." Mirabel frantically looks around, from the intact walls to the crowd of wide-eyed faces.

Abuela clears her throat and steps forward. She stands at the railing overlooking the courtyard and the crowd. "There is nothing wrong with la Casa Madrigal," she announces. Her voice is strong and yet soothing. I can feel the crowd relaxing, grateful Abuela is in charge. "The magic is strong! Please! Return to the fiesta. Eat! Drink! Disfrutan! Enjoy Antonio's animals and his new gift."

Abuela sweeps through the crowd, taking Antonio forward so that he's the center of attention again. As he should be.

Mirabel is stone. Glued to the floor.

My sigh is almost as deep as Abuela's. Before I go downstairs, I reach out to touch Mirabel's sleeve. "Why can't you just be happy for him?" I ask.

My sister doesn't answer. I'm not sure what to

do. I want to comfort her because that's my duty as the oldest sister, but I don't want Abuela to be angry with me, too. I want to ask Mirabel what she was thinking, but I don't want the guests to think I believe her nonsense. I withdraw my hand and turn to follow the others, leaving my sister alone with her fantasies.

Chapter 7 * Mirabel

IT'S COZY IN THE KITCHEN, where I'm sitting nibbling on one of the arepas that Mamá is making. The cheesy goodness warms my heart, which is what it's supposed to do. But I still feel grumpy.

"The cracks were real," I say, my mouth full. "They were all over."

Mamá nods but doesn't look up from working the masa.

"If it was all in my head, how did I cut my hand?"

When she saw my cut, she made me come to the kitchen for her cure.

"I would never ruin Antonio's big night!" I slump in my chair. Antonio is probably my favorite Madrigal. He's always been my best friend. I think of him in his new room—and me in my lonely, unmagical one. Even though I'm sad, I would never do anything to hurt my cousin. "Is that really what you think?"

Mamá wipes her hands on her apron and brushes her hair out of her face, leaving a white floury mess. "What I think is that tonight was very hard for you—"

"It's not that!" I can't help raising my voice, even though it's not her fault. If only someone else had seen the cracks. If only Casita could show them to the family. If only someone—anyone—believed me. But because I don't have a gift, why would they? "I said I was fine!"

"Amor, you're not. Or tonight would have . . ." She watches me like I'm a small child who doesn't understand anything. She looks at me like she pities me. "Or tonight would have turned out differently."

She leaves the stove and takes my hand, examining the healing wound carefully. "Why are you always injuring yourself, Mirabel?"

I don't answer, because I know it's the kind of question that doesn't need one. I'm always doing everything wrong even when I try to do things right. I want to be good like Isabela, to obey like Luisa. But I can't. All I want is to be part of this family. Even though Felix and my papá don't have gifts either, they're more a part of the family than I am. I mean, everyone loves to hear my dad play the piano, and Felix is always cracking people up. Besides, they have each other. I have . . . no one. My nose drips, and I use my free arm to swipe my sleeve across my face. If Isabela saw me do that, she'd think I was gross. She always uses a handkerchief.

Mamá doesn't notice, though. "I was looking out for the family," I say. We both watch the blood slowly dry and fade from my hand. "I might not be super strong like Luisa or effortlessly perfect like Señorita Perfecta Isabela, who's never had a bad hair day." I eye the flour in Mamá's hair. I wonder for a second if Mamá has bad hair days like I do. Actually, I think as I study Mamá's hair some more, the flour looks kind of nice with her streaks of gray, almost like it was on purpose. Nope, I'm the only one with bad hair days.

"Whatever," I sigh.

"I wish you could see yourself the way I do," Mamá says, still holding my hand. "You are perfect just like this." She reaches up and smooths my hair. We both have wild curls that refuse to be tamed. "You are just as special as anyone else in this family."

I raise one eyebrow, looking first at my hand—good as new—and then at Mamá. "You just healed my hand with an arepa con queso."

Mamá laughs and shakes her head. "I just healed your hand with my love." She pulls me toward her. Is she going to make me sit on her lap? I'm fifteen—way too old for that! "My love for my daughter, with her wonderful brain—"

"Ugh! Here we go." I try to wiggle away.

"—big heart—"

"Mamá!"

"—cool glasses!"

"Argh!" I sputter as she plants a wet kiss on my cheek.

"Ay," she says, gazing at me. Her eyes are dark pools, like she wants to understand me but can't. "Te amo, cosa linda."

I know she loves me, but I'm not a little kid anymore. I shrug off her hug.

"I know what I saw."

Mamá sighs and shakes her head, wiping her

hands on a dish towel. "Mira, my brother, Bruno, lost his way in this family." She reaches up and tucks a strand of hair behind my ear. "I don't want the same for you. Get some sleep. You'll feel better tomorrow."

But I know I won't let this go. I can't.

Everyone else is spending the night swaying in Antonio's jungle room, but I return to my nursery. I'd just be in the way there. I open my door, and the nursery looks plainer than ever. Even my pathetic attempts at decorating—the stitching, the drawings—look sad. But I know I didn't make up those cracks. I didn't dream up the fading candle. I saw what I saw.

I crawl into bed, but it's obvious I'm not getting any sleep tonight, no matter what Mama told me. There's no way I'm sleeping, not with everything going on in my head. I *know* those cracks mean something. And it can't be good.

I throw off the covers and get out of bed. My bedroom door creaks as I open it and look across the courtyard at the candle in Abuela's window. I tiptoe out of my room. As I head toward Abuela's room, I run my hand along the corridor wall. Smooth. No cracks.

Clink. Ca-chink.

I hear Abuela's chatelaine as I near her room. Through the window, in the glow of the candle, I can see Abuela. She paces her room, and the keys and trinkets on her chatelaine jangle with each step. Her room is simple with a plain bed. Even though everyone else has amazing rooms like Antonio, Abuela's room is basic, no frills. The furniture seems old, the bedspread worn. I wonder if these are the same things she brought with her when she first arrived at the Encanto. I hear a noise—something like a cough or a wheeze—and study her face . . . I'm not sure what's happening. I've never seen her face do this. . . . I squint and realize she's crying. Proud, strong, stoic Abuela is crying! This cannot be good. Abuela grabs the locket that hangs from her chatelaine. She clicks it open, and I catch a glimpse of the sepia photograph of my abuelo.

"Ay, Pedro," Abuela says, gazing at the photo.

I jump back into the shadows.

"Ay, what do I do?" Abuela says, her voice soft and sad. "If anyone knew how vulnerable we truly are, how quickly our home could be lost. Bruno knew that cracks would grow, that our magic might falter, and he kept it from us."

An icy cold goes up my spine. *Bruno? Our magic might falter?* This is not good.

"And now I need help, mi amor," she says. I try to imagine Abuela as a young woman. It's hard, but as she looks at her husband's picture, I can almost visualize the bride she was fifty years ago. It's strange to see how people look when they don't think they're being watched.

"I need some way to keep our home from breaking." I've never heard Abuela ask for help before. She always seems so strong, like someone who would never, ever need help from anyone. I wish I could reach out to her, but I keep silent in the shadows outside her window. "If the truth can be found, help me find it. Help me protect our family." Her words are like a prayer. Abuela raises the locket to her lips. "Help me save our miracle." Instead of kissing the locket, she snaps it shut.

My heart is pounding so loud I'm lucky it doesn't wake Dolores. I can feel the sting of a tear in my eye. I wish I could help Abuela as I watch her huddled figure.

Abuela wipes her eyes and stares at the candle. The wax drips. The cracks I saw were real. The fading candle—that was real, too. I didn't imagine any of it. I'm not a troublemaker! I'm not crazy! I stand up taller, straighter. If I was the only one who saw the cracks, maybe that means I can help Abuela. I need to help her. I need to save the magic. I need to save the family. My family.

I will help my strong, powerful, sometimes scary

abuela. I'm sure I didn't imagine those cracks. I was shown those cracks for a *reason*. I've got to help my grandmother *and* the rest of my family. *This is it*, I think. I'm going to save the miracle. Protect my family. My house. Casita nudges me down the hallway as if encouraging me.

"I will find a way!" I say as confidently as I can. "I will save the miracle!"

My whole life I've wanted to prove I'm more than what everyone sees. And now is my chance. I will make them proud.

Casita's shutters squeak as they open and close, as if the house isn't so sure.

I shake my head. "I have no idea how to save a miracle," I tell Casita.

On the other hand, there *is* one person in this family who hears all the secrets around here. And that's just where I'll start.

Chapter 8 * Luisa

WOW, THAT WAS SOME PARTY! Antonio's room was the perfect spot to celebrate his day— and night. My room isn't quite as exciting as a whole jungle filled with gorgeous and friendly animals. My room is a maze of weights and pulleys. There are ropes to climb, bars to swing across, and a shower to clean me up: everything a girl like me could need. I don't remember the family having that much fun on *my* gift day. Mostly everyone wanted to watch me do tricks with my brand-new strength. You know—lifting heavy things, moving houses and churches, digging deep holes. Honestly, I felt a little like a performer at a circus. I still do, actually. I know it's important to use our gifts to help the family, but a girl gets tired sometimes.

I yawn and stretch. And I somehow manage to fall out of bed. Boy, am I tired this morning.

"Breakfast!" Mamá calls.

And I'm starving.

I stumble up and quickly get dressed. It doesn't matter so much what I wear, as long as I'm comfortable. I don't think someone like Isabela can appreciate the need for clothing that allows for movement. I stand in front of my mirror and flex my biceps. Yes, this blouse is perfect.

Downstairs, the whole family is making its usual racket, although I notice the parents are drinking more café than usual. Everyone is talking about Antonio's party, and the boy of the day himself is bouncing around between his uncle and cousins, telling them all about his new animal friends. Antonio never used to talk this much. That's what a gift does—makes you more confident about who you are. I smile.

I head over to fill my plate. The huevos look delicious.

Dolores is right behind me with an overflowing plate of food. For someone so birdlike, she sure can eat.

"Dolores, hey!" We turn around and see Mirabel.

Here we go. I'm not the only one a little annoyed with her this morning. The moment Tía Pepa sees Mirabel, clouds form overhead. *Uh-oh.* When Isabela walks by with her café con leche, Mirabel reaches out, but Isabela flounces away, her pretty, delicate sleeves fluttering. See, I would ruin a fancy dress like that. A few cute little hummingbirds hover over Isabela's head. *Aw, I wish little birds hung around me.*

"You know," Mirabel says to Dolores, "out of all my older cousins, you're, like, my favorite cousin." I watch Dolores to see if she realizes that she's Mirabel's *only* older cousin. "So I feel like I can talk to you about anything." Mirabel continues to load Dolores's plate with more food. "Ergo, you can talk to *me* about anything. Like the problem with the magic last night that no one seemed to know about?" Mirabel winks at Dolores. "But maybe someone secretly knows about?"

"Camilo!" my tío Felix calls from the table. "Stop pretending to be Dolores just so you can have seconds."

Mirabel and I look at Dolores, who shape-shifts into Camilo. "Worth a shot, eh!" He heads back to his seat with his full plate.

The real Dolores budges in line and whispers in Mirabel's ear. "The only one worried about the magic is you," she says. "And the rats, counting in the walls."

I wrinkle my face at Dolores. *Rats in the walls?*

Her hearing might be a little too good. Yeesh! I'm glad I can't hear that!

Dolores looks at Mirabel and then back at me. "And Luisa."

I freeze. Busted?

"I heard her sweating all night."

Mirabel stares at me, opens her mouth to speak.

"Everyone get to the table!" Abuela declares, interrupting whatever was going to happen next. "Let's go, let's go. Vámanos." Anyone who hasn't found a seat yet sits obediently. I'm stuck next to Mirabel.

"Luisa—" Mirabel whispers.

"Family, we are all thankful for Antonio's wonderful gift," Abuela continues. She pulls out her chair at the head of the table only to be greeted by the chirping of a few coatis.

Antonio giggles. "I told them to warm up your seat!"

Abuela shoos them away. "Thank you, Toñito. I'm sure today we'll find a way to put your blessing to good use." The coatis jump and leap from Abuela's chair to the table and then onto her shoulder.

"Luisa," Mirabel hisses in my ear as our grandmother struggles with Antonio's animals. "Did you talk to Abuela last night? About something secret?"

I try so hard to keep a neutral expression. Straight line for my mouth. Open, honest eyes. No blushing or flushing. Ears . . . what are ears supposed to do?

"You did!" Mirabel gasps. She pounds the table in excitement.

Now my ears are turning red. That's what they do, I guess.

"Mirabel!" Abuela says, finally rid of the coatis. "If you can't pay attention, I will help you."

I can tell Mirabel is working on making her expression neutral now. And she isn't any better at it than I am.

"Casita," Abuela calls. Instantly, Casita yanks Mirabel's chair away from mine.

What a relief.

"As I was saying, we must work every day to earn our miracle. So today we will work twice as hard."

Mirabel raises her hand. "I'll help Luisa—"

"Wait," Abuela says sternly. If I were Mirabel, I would keep quiet. Abuela seems to be losing patience. "First, an announcement. I've spoken to the Guzmáns and we'll be moving up Isabela's engagement to Mariano."

I glance at my sister. She looks . . . nervous?

But Abuela continues. "Dolores, do we have a new time?"

Dolores cocks her head like an owl listening. "Tonight," she says. "He wants five babies. . . ."

Yikes. Isa sprouts a few nervous daisies. Abuela's eyes dart to Dolores. My cousin stops talking.

"Such a fine young man with our perfect Isabela will bring a new generation of blessings and make both of our families stronger." Abuela smiles as if she can see a rosy future. Isabela smiles a perfect smile. I tilt my head and study her face. Is her smile a little *too* perfect? Does she look like she's trying a little *too* hard? I wonder what Isa thinks of the whole thing.

"Kissy, kissy!" Smooching sounds come from the other end of the room. Someone who looks just like Mariano is puckering up. Then Mariano shifts back into Camilo, who howls with laughter. I can't help laughing when Antonio falls off his chair from giggling so much.

"Okay, our community is counting on us. Get out there," Abuela continues. "Go make your family proud."

"Make the family proud," we all repeat in unison.

Mirabel jumps out of her seat like a rocket and runs into Isabela, who frowns. "Watch the hair," she says and swishes her locks.

I watch my sisters. Wouldn't want to get on the wrong side of either of them.

"Luisa—"

I jump up and leave the dining room before my

nosy sister can ask any more questions. Besides, I have work to do.

Abuela's idea of making the family proud, at least for me, is moving a church in town. The padre looks on as I set it down. "Uh, a little to the left, Luisa?" I pick it up again.

"No, how about to the right?"

I stifle a sigh. My job is to help the community, I remind myself. "Sure, got it!" I say and move the church again.

"Gracias, Luisa. Que Dios te bendiga," the priest says.

"Luisa!" I hear. It's Señora Osma, who always wants something. "Can you reroute the river?"

I brush off my hands and paste a smile on my face. "Will do!" I say, even though that's the last thing I have time for today.

"Uh, Luisa," says Señor Rendon, who is sometimes careless, "the donkeys got out again."

"On it," I confirm. But I can't help wondering why Señor Rendon doesn't keep better track of the donkeys.

"So, Luisa—" Mirabel calls after me as I head toward the runaway donkeys. No one dawdles when Abuela asks them to do something. *Help the family, help the family.* I don't stop. *Reroute the river. Find the donkeys.* I have my own work to do. I walk faster—which is pretty fast. Mirabel starts running. "Wait! Luisa!"

"Luisa!" Out of nowhere appears Señora Ruiz. "Doña Alma said you could repave the plaza."

The plaza? Didn't I do that last year? I think. But I don't say anything. I just nod. "No problem."

I pick up two donkeys and bring them back to Señor Rendon. Oh, just great! One of the donkeys does its business all over my shoe. *Gross!*

"Luisa!"

Who is calling my name now? I look back and see Mirabel. Again. "I'm kind of busy," I say as nicely as possible, even though I grit my teeth. As if she shouldn't be able to tell that. She's always so caught up in her own world.

"Yeah, I hear you. But, um, wait a minute." I glare at her. And yet she keeps talking. "What's going on with the magic?" She looks at me with pleading eyes.

"Magic's fine." I scrape my shoe on a rock. "Just got a lotta chores, so maybe you should go home—"

"If you tell me," Mirabel insists, "maybe I can help. . . ."

I head toward the river.

"Luisa," Señora Flores says as I pass her house, "my house is leaning to the . . ."

Without looking at Señora Flores and without missing a step, I shove her house into position again.

"Luisa? You're lying." Mirabel is like a little dog yapping at my ankles. "Dolores said you were sweating all night, and you never sweat, so you must—"

"Move," I say as I scoop up another of Señor Rendon's runaways. "You're going to make me drop a donkey." *On you,* I think but don't say.

"Will you just—Luisa!" Mirabel says. "You say yes to everyone but your sister who never asks for anything, even though everything is easy for you. But when I need you, the most stupid donkeys are more important than your own family!"

I stop dead in my tracks. The donkey I'm carrying gives a little grunt. "Don't worry about it." The donkey brays.

"Just tell me what you know." Mirabel looks around, even though the townspeople are busy with their own chores. It's just the two of us. And the donkey.

"Luisa? You're obviously nervous about something. Is it about last night? Luisa, if you know something, and you don't say, and it gets worse—"

"I felt something!" I yell at her.

"Felt what? Something to do with the magic?"

She's staring at me. I shake my head. "I didn't. On second thought, I didn't." I hoist the donkey I'm carrying higher. "There were no cracks. I'm good, everything's good. I'm not nervous."

Mirabel will not stop staring. Her eyes behind her green glasses are huge and unblinking. "Luisa?"

"I'm *not* nervous!" I can feel my face turning red. She blinks.

I set down the donkey—on top of a boulder, but never mind about that. "Argh!" I groan. I can't believe I let my sister see me break down.

"Okay, okay." Mirabel backs away. "I'm not saying you are. I mean, because you're . . . you . . ."

"Listen, it's just that Abuela was already all over me, and now I've got to pave a river and dig a plaza." Or was it the other way around? I sigh. "No one gets it! They only see what's on the surface." I hold out my shoe. It smells terrible. "And see this?"

Mirabel makes a face. She agrees that it's disgusting. And for some reason, the look on her face—a combination of embarrassment, a bit of pity, and barely contained nervous laughter—makes me want to tell her what it's like.

"No one thinks I might get crushed under this weight."

"You?" Mirabel's eyes pop open.

"Not actual weight. I mean, I'm strong. But the pressure of having to do everything. To do everything for everyone. I never get to relax, never get to just have fun." I try to explain to Mirabel that even a strong girl like me can get tired. Tired of the responsibilities and the expectations. She nods like maybe she agrees, although there's no way she can understand what it's like to have everyone counting on you.

"I really think you need a break, Luisa," she says.

I'm panting, but it sure felt good to, well,

explode. It felt good to tell Mirabel what it's really like for me. I shake my head. "Luisa doesn't take breaks."

I give her a hug. And then I squeeze harder.

"Suffocating," she says from inside my hug. She's fine, I think, and squeeze harder.

Maybe I should help her out. "You want to find a secret about the magic? Go to Bruno's tower," I tell her. "Find his last vision."

Mirabel mumbles something I can't understand. Perhaps the hug is a bit too tight. I loosen my grip a little. "Vision?" she repeats. "Vision of what?"

"No one knows," I say. "They never found it."

Mirabel squirms out of my arms. She looks surprised. I'm not sure if it's surprise about the vision or surprise about me and what I just said.

"Luisa!" someone calls. "The donkeys!"

I look around for the donkeys. Ugh, they're all over the place again. "I'm on it!" I call, and pick up a donkey.

"I'm serious about you taking a break," Mirabel says, like she really means it. Maybe my little sister isn't so bad.

"You're a good one, Sis." I give her a sock in the arm. "Maybe I will!" I say with a smile.

"Wait!" Mirabel cries. "How do you 'find' a vision? What does that even mean?"

With a donkey under my arm, I head toward the plaza again. Reroute the plaza, pave the river. No. Pave the river, reroute the plaza. Got it.

I stop and turn back. "You'll know when you find it," I tell Mirabel. "You're a good listener, Sis. Let's do that again." I hoist the donkey in my arm. "But be careful," I call after her. "That place is off-limits for a reason."

Chapter 9 * Mirabel

I'VE GOT THIS. I'll be fine. I've got this. I'll be fine.

This is my mantra as I return home to "find the vision," whatever that means. Luisa was . . . odd. But she was sort of helpful. I mean, she told me her secret, along with a lot of other stuff I didn't know about her. I can't believe that she gets tired of all the responsibilities. She makes everything look so easy!

Nothing ever seems to be easy for me. But: *I've got this. I'll be fine.* My plan—if you can call it that—is to go to Bruno's tower and . . . well, I haven't thought that far yet. I sling my mochila over my shoulder and head toward the staircase. As I slip through the courtyard, I hear voices.

"Yes," Abuela is saying to someone. I peek around the corner and see her put her arm through Isabela's.

"I can't think of a more perfect match," Isabela says. I'm not sure why she wants to get married already. She's twenty-two, which is definitely old enough to get married, but also kind of young. I mean, Mariano is handsome and everything, but she's got plenty of time. Not that I would ever say that to *her*—or Abuela. I head toward Bruno's room without them seeing me.

As I climb toward Bruno's door, I look up at Abuela's window. I can see the candle, but the flame sputters. It's definitely not as bright as it used to be. There's no time to lose. I keep going, faster, huffing and puffing. If I were as strong as Luisa, I wouldn't be breathing this hard. If I were as perfect as Isabela, I probably wouldn't be in this mess, whatever it is.

I keep climbing. The higher I climb, the taller each stair feels. My legs burn and my breath is short. At last, I clear off the cobwebs before I pry open Bruno's door with a cranky creak.

The entrance to Bruno's room is so dim I can't see anything at first. I stand in the darkness as, little by little, shapes form around me. "Achoo!" I wipe my nose with my sleeve. It's very dusty in here. As my eyes adjust, I see that it's not just dusty—it's sandy. Sand spills from above in a curtain, making little sand dunes everywhere.

"Casita, can you turn off the sand?" I call. But the sand continues to flow.

The floor tiles outside Bruno's room flip and flop, as if in answer to my question.

"You . . . you can't help in here?"

No, the house seems to tell me.

 99

My blood goes cold. I've never been on my own before. I mean, I'm often *alone*—I'm the only Madrigal without a gift, after all. But I'm never totally *on my own*. I always have Casita.

"Uh," I say. My voice sounds tinny and timid. "I'll be fine. I need to do this." I take a deep breath as if I could breathe in courage. "I need to do this for you, Casa. For Abuela. And, I guess, for me, too."

My shoes make a gritty sound as I take a few steps forward into the dark room.

"Okay," I say aloud. "Find the vision." My voice echoes in the strange space. I take a few more steps. *I've got this. I'll be fine.* It can't be that bad. I'm not scared, I remind myself. "Save the mirac—"

Instead of stepping on floor tiles, I find myself stepping into . . . nothing. And there go my feet! I'm sliding now, slipping through the sand. I come to rest at the bottom of a sand dune. I have sand in my eyes and my mouth and a lot of other places you should never have sand.

The room is huge, of course, like everyone's room (well, except for the nursery). Only even bigger. Like, gigantic. There's a steep, rocky mountain face.

There is a magnificent waterfall.

Only—wait, it's not a waterfall. It's a *sandfall!* More stairs wind their way up to the top of the rock face, where something glows green. And pointing toward the stairs is a huge sign that says VISIONS!

I look from the green glowing room to the sign to the stairs. "Guess I'm getting my exercise today," I say to myself. Then I laugh since there's no one else around to appreciate my joke.

Croak, croak! I duck as Antonio's toucan swoops awkwardly toward me. Is that a smile I see on the bird's face?

"Huh," I say to the toucan. "Lotta stairs." I crane my neck to see how far and how many. "But at least I won't have to climb them alone." I gesture to the toucan to go first. But it croak-laughs and flies away. Or maybe I will.

I'll be fine. I've got this.

If I thought I was tired after the first flight of stairs, I'm completely outdone now. Each step is like hot pokers in my calves. My shoes feel like wooden boards. My chest tightens with each inhale.

Croak! The toucan perches near me as I pause to try to catch my breath. I shake my head. "We meet again," I pant. "Any ideas for making this easier? Not all of us can fly."

The toucan doesn't answer but hops back and forth on the railing. Only, I realize, it's not any old railing. It's a rope. *I've got this!* I fling the rope over a boulder at the top of the sandfall. There must be a way to swing myself up like one of Antonio's coatis. I grab hold of the rope, take a step back, squeeze my eyes shut, and hurl myself into the glowing green space.

This part of Bruno's room is a disaster. Weird pictures line the walls—are those the visions? There's sand everywhere, like he's never owned a broom. Jagged edges of emeralds poke out here and there, giving the space its green glow. In one corner I spot a rat—no, four rats—emerging from an old, broken jug. I look up and see a sculpture of my tío. But it's odd because his eyes are scratched out. Rats crawl in and out of the spot where his eyes should be. Talk about creepy.

A scratched-up sculpture and rats. Is this the vision? I don't see how any of this will help save the house, the magic, the family. I hear a creak and a croak. The toucan eyes the next room, where the noise came from, and flies away.

"Quitter," I say. Although, honestly, if I could fly, I might be gone, too.

Instead, I move forward. Must save the magic.

The family. The Encanto. I walk toward the glow, deeper into Bruno's inner sanctum. But when I enter the dark room, it's empty. Just a circle of sand.

"There's nothing here," I say, my words echoing in the space. "After all that work?" I collapse on the floor. Who cares if my clothes get sandy? I'm not the perfect one.

I sit cross-legged with my elbows on my knees. What now? I look down and brush away the sand. Something glows brightly beneath the surface. "What is it?"

It's another emerald, but it's somehow different from the other green rocks. I keep digging. Pretty soon I can see it's another sculpture—a piece of a picture. Is this Bruno's vision?

I crawl around, dusting off shards. These must be from his vision, but they're all smashed. It's almost impossible to tell what they are. I pick up a shard of emerald. And another. They're like puzzle pieces, each with their own unique jagged edges and weird pictures. I grab two shards and try to fit them together. Nope, not those. I pick up another one. A perfect fit. The two pieces form part of a picture.

"What does it mean?" I squint at it. Something seems familiar.

"It's me!" I startle and drop the shards. "It's my face! Am I part of Bruno's vision?"

I pick up one piece and then another. And another. These might be important. I drop them into my mochila just in case. Suddenly, the whole tower seems to shake. No, wait, it *is* shaking. I look around. There are cracks everywhere now, sand falling through all of them. I grab more shards as they scatter in the sand that gushes, runs like rivers. I'm like a floating piece of driftwood getting carried by the tide of sand. I cling to my mochila and snatch shards of green as they whirl past me. At last I see the door—an exit. I manage to pull myself up and grip the handle.

It's locked!

Sand is piling up behind me. It's going to bury

me. There's nowhere to turn. I have to get through this door! I hitch my mochila higher on my shoulder. *I'll be fine.*

I jiggle the handle. *I've got this.*

Whoosh! Along with a tidal wave of sand, I plunge through the door.

Chapter 10 * Luisa

SOMETHING IS NOT RIGHT. I feel . . . strange. One minute I was finishing up with the plaza and the next, I had the overwhelming urge for a nap. And I never nap! Nighttime is for sleeping, I always say. Daytime is for getting things done.

But this afternoon, I couldn't resist closing my eyes for a few moments, especially once Señor Rendon's donkeys were back where they belong.

When I opened my eyes, they were loose again! And the river . . . oh, Abuela is going to be so mad at me.

I drag myself toward home. In the courtyard, I see Camilo playing soccer with the Casa. Besides fooling his family by shape-shifting into different people, playing soccer with Casita is Camilo's favorite activity. He plays in the courtyard, and the stairs become the goal. He kicks the ball and the steps shoot it back again. The sound of the slapping of the ball and Camilo's laughter is a pretty normal thing we hear in this house. Now, though, it makes me tired just watching the ball zoom toward him. It seems faster than usual.

"Slow down, Casita!" Camilo shouts. The ball torpedoes toward him, and when he glances up to see Mirabel, it knocks him in the head. "Ouch!"

That's not like Casita at all. The house is always very gentle when we play. At least, that's what I remember from back when I had time to play.

"Mirabel! Careful." Mirabel has just come

around the corner on the second floor and smacked right into Abuela. Casita would usually help us avoid that kind of collision by gently guiding one or the other around. Abuela drops her chatelaine with a clatter. And Mirabel drops something from her mochila.

"I'm sorry, I'm sorry," babbles Mirabel. She kneels, scooping up whatever she dropped. "I was just, uh, everything's fine. I'm normal."

Normal? That's exactly what it's not. Fine? Definitely not.

"Where are you coming from in such a hurry?" Abuela asks Mirabel.

Where *is* she coming from? I wonder. Did she find the vision? I slump on a large stone in the courtyard. Does her finding the vision have anything to do with how strange I feel? Oh, how I wish I hadn't said anything to her. I should have kept my mouth shut! But it felt so good to be honest about how I feel.

"I was just, um . . ." Mirabel says.

I stand up. I shake out my arms, crack my neck. I'm probably getting worked up over nothing. If everything is okay, I tell myself, I'll be able to lift this stone. It's nothing. I've moved it a million times. No one can ever decide where it looks best. I bend down, wrap my arms around its rough edges. And heave—

"My gift!" I shriek. I cannot lift the stone. It feels like—well, like stone. It's *heavy*. Is this what it feels like to be normal? Like Mirabel? This can't be happening!

I hear Abuela's footsteps hurry along the balcony and down the stairs. "Luisa?"

"I'm losing my gift!" I stop trying to lift the stone and sit on it again. I slump over and put my head in my hands.

"What do you mean?" Mirabel kneels in front of me, laying her hands on my arms, and Abuela stands with a worried look on her face. "What?"

"I was supposed to be helping the town," I sob, "and I took a break." Mirabel gasps. I nod and continue, "I knew it was wrong, but I fell asleep. And I woke up and the river was flooding because I hadn't rerouted it yet. And I knew I let *you* down."

I grab Abuela's hand. "Then the donkeys were in the corn and I tried to fix it, but they were so heavy. . . ."

I demonstrate, tugging and pulling the stone. My brow is damp with the sweat of exertion. Or panic.

Abuela eyes Mirabel. "Did you say something to her?"

"I, uh, just . . ."

I know Abuela is worried, too.

I can't listen anymore. I know it's rude and I know it's childish, but I run toward my room.

"Were you with her today?" I hear Abuela ask Mirabel as I dash up the stairs. But before my little sister can answer, the bells from the church ring loudly, signaling the time. Abuela clears her throat. "The Guzmáns are expecting me," she says. "Tell no one."

Tell no one? I think as I open my door.

"There's nothing wrong with Luisa," Abuela says soothingly to Mirabel. *I can't even lift a stupid stone!* But I wonder if she is saying it to convince herself, too. "We can't have the family in a panic. Tonight is too important."

Panic? I slam my door shut. Now I *know* I should start panicking.

Chapter 11 * Mirabel

THAT WAS A CLOSE CALL! When I ran into
Abuela, a bunch of the pieces of Bruno's vision fell
from my mochila. I almost couldn't grab the last
one without Abuela noticing. It was right next to
her skirt! If she found out what I had in my bag, I
know I would be in big trouble. But I'm not afraid.
I think of what I witnessed with Luisa. Imagine:
Luisa without her strength? Luisa crying? I have

to get back to my room and look through all the shards of Bruno's vision. I need to put them all together. I need to figure out what they mean. I need to make the Familia Madrigal proud.

Back in the nursery, I collapse on my bed. The springs squeak. I feel so mixed up. Luisa getting tired? The sand in Bruno's tower? Abuela—well, Abuela seems pretty normal, actually. But why is my face part of Bruno's vision?

I sit up and straighten the bedspread, dumping the shards of his vision across my bed like a puzzle. I move the pieces around. If only I could make sense of them. I close my eyes. "Why am I in your vision, Bruno?" I ask aloud. Maybe when I open my eyes, I'll be able to see what I'm missing.

Instead, what I see when I open them is Tía Pepa standing in the doorway to the nursery, a thundercloud overhead.

"Geez, Tía," I say, trying to rearrange myself so that the pieces of Bruno's vision aren't so obvious.

"Sorry, I just wanted to get the last of Antonio's

things, and then I heard"—Tía Pepa is distracted briefly by the rain that starts dripping on her head before she finishes her sentence—"'the name we do not speak.'"

The moment "name" escapes her mouth, Pepa is soaked. A thunderclap rumbles. "Great, now I'm drizzling," she says, "and a drizzle will lead to a sprinkle and a sprinkle will lead to a shower and a . . ." She shoos away the dripping cloud with her hand, trying to push it out my bedroom door. "Clear skies, clear skies, clear skies."

Pretty soon, Pepa's mantra seems to work its magic and the rain clouds disappear. I squint at her.

"Tía Pepa," I say. "If Bru—I mean, if *he* had a vision about someone, what would it mean?"

My aunt picks up a pair of Antonio's underwear from the far corner of the nursery. She scoops up a box filled with shells from under his bed. She finds one of his sandals under the window and the other one behind the door. I have the distinct feeling she's not answering me.

"Pepa . . . ?"

"Mira, we need to get ready for the Guzmáns tonight. Isabela's special night." She straightens her lips into a line.

I open my mouth to protest.

"Mira, please." The rain cloud above her head is gathering once again, getting darker and thicker and rainier. I don't want to upset her, but I need to understand.

"I know, but it's just that, um, hypothetically . . ." I can't look at her while I'm asking this. She's not looking at me, either. She's standing at the window clutching the random little-boy belongings in her arms. I take a deep breath and plunge. "If he saw you in one of his visions, was it generally positive?"

"It was a nightmare!"

Both Pepa and I jump at the voice.

"Felix!" Pepa exclaims. My tío's standing at the door, his usually smiling face serious. She shoots him a look.

"She needs to know, Pepi," my uncle says. "She

needs to know." Felix sits on the bed that used to be his son's. "He ruined everything."

I think of the dunes of sand, the ugly boulders, the dust and rats. "Ruined how?"

"Well—"

"We don't talk about Bruno." Pepa hugs the shoes and underwear tighter.

"He'd get in your mind," Felix continues. "He'd show you something terrible. And, bing-bang-boom, it would happen."

"We don't talk about Bruno!" My poor aunt is a walking thunderstorm now. But I still need to know.

"What if you didn't understand what you saw?" I ask Felix.

"Then you'd better figure it out, because it was coming for you!"

Chapter 12 * Isabela

I'M TENDING THE BRIGHT pink bougainvillea outside my bedroom when I hear it. The name we do not speak. Who is talking about him? I slip out of my room. Abuela will be so mad if she hears about this, and I don't want to upset her. As I hurry along the balcony, I hear the crash of thunder. Is Tía Pepa talking about my uncle?

I run toward the noise. Of course, it's coming

from Mirabel's room. When will she stop looking for trouble? I peer around the nursery door and see my sister on her bed, a mess of junk spilling out of her mochila, dirtying her bedspread. Pepa, followed by a storm cloud and the occasional burst of lightning, is talking to her. Felix chimes in every so often.

"We don't talk about Bruno!" Pepa shouts.

Why are they saying the name we do not speak? I want to hush her in case Abuela is nearby. But I don't want them to know I'm here, listening. I'm the perfect one, the one who never gets in trouble, never upsets Abuela. Or anyone else.

"Our wedding day!" wails Pepa. "Remember, Felix, mi amor?"

Felix puts an arm around his wife, not even noticing the drizzle. Watching them together reminds me of the photos of their wedding. Pepa in a beautiful white dress and lace mantilla. Felix in his suit and tie, his hair slicked back with pomade. They were a perfect couple.

Mamá told me that the morning of their wedding was gorgeous—sunny, bright, not a cloud in the sky. But then, she said, a little puffy one appeared. Bruno took his sister's hand, pointed at the sky, and said, "It looks like rain." Everyone laughed. Until it began to sprinkle. Then rain. The wind picked up; the palm trees swayed. Mamá said her favorite hat—one with peacock feathers—flew off her head and wasn't found until two weeks later (on the head of a mischievous chigüiro). Pretty soon it was a hurricane, a tornado. Pepa and Felix had their wedding in a downpour, the cake soaked, the champagne watery, the dancing damp—they didn't let Bruno's vision ruin it completely. But it was not the happy day it should have been.

Everyone talked about his vision after that. *Bruno says it looks like rain and then it rains!* It didn't help that, for a while, the townspeople wouldn't stop talking about his visions. Papá told me that Bruno told Señora Osma that her fish would die—and it did! A sad little goldfish floating upside down in a fishbowl. Mamá told me that Señora Uriarte was told by Bruno that her hair would go gray. If you see her in town, you can tell it's her by the coil of gray-white hair piled on her head. Pepa once said that Bruno told the donkey delivery guy that he would grow a gut. I've never known him *without* a round belly. Everything that Bruno said came true.

"Bruno was always right," I blurt. Mirabel, Pepa, and Felix all turn to look at me.

"We don't talk about Bruno!" Pepa says. And then she adds, "What was it he told you?"

"Well," I say carefully, and then mumble under my breath about how I was promised to someday have the life of my dreams.

Mirabel looks up from the mess on her bed to roll her eyes at me. I mean, I don't blame her; that actually sounds like a pretty good vision. But you never know with Bruno's visions.

"Well," says Pepa, "Mariano *is* on his way here tonight."

"He also told me," I continue, "that my power

would increase." As I say this, a spattering of purple and white lilies sprout around me and their petals flutter to the ground like delicate butterflies.

"Well," someone says. It's Dolores, appearing out of nowhere. As usual. I wonder how far away she was when she heard us talking about Bruno. "He told me that the man I've always dreamed about will be beyond my reach."

"What?" Tía Pepa says and hugs her daughter. I feel sorry for Dolores. She's old enough to be married, but how sad to be told that the man of your dreams is taken. I give her the saddest, most sympathetic look I can. I'm glad that wasn't his vision for *me*. "I'm sorry Bruno saw that, mija," Pepa says. Another cloud gathers above her head. Dolores sniffles.

"Did someone say Bruno?"

We all stare, wide-eyed, as Bruno himself strides into the room—and then shifts into the shape of Camilo.

"Camilo!" we cry in unison.

"I forgot the rats," Camilo says, a grin on his face. "Of course, rats or no rats, he sure was scary." Camilo shifts back into our hunched-over uncle, his face pale, circles under his eyes. This time a gray rat scurries up the specter's hooded poncho. And then, just as quickly, Camilo shifts into the tall shape of Mariano—tall and handsome, dark haired and blue-eyed. Responsible, dependable, and definitely in love with me. Everyone says. "By the way, Isabela," Camilo says in Mariano's voice, "your boyfriend's downstairs."

"Camilo!" I snap, wanting to lunge for him, but keeping myself contained.

Camilo shifts back to himself again and howls with laughter as he races out of the room.

I think of Mariano—the real one—waiting downstairs. Why does it feel so far away? "I guess I'd better go. . . ."

I trail off as I hear something. We all fall silent, listening. It doesn't take superhuman hearing to know what the jingling, jangling sound means.

"Did someone say *Mariano*, mi amor?" Abuela approaches, her chatelaine of keys and trinkets clanking. She wraps an arm around my waist and squeezes. Sometimes Abuela seems standoffish and maybe even a tiny bit mean, but when she hugs you or smiles at you, it's like the world gets bigger. You feel safe and loved. All you want to do is make Abuela happy so that you can be in her embrace again. "You must be so excited, Isabela. I know this is the big night. The proposal, mi amor."

Mirabel drops something on the floor with a clatter. She crawls under her bed to retrieve whatever nonsense she's playing with. She's too old for toys. I look around the sad little nursery. I can barely remember my few years in here. She's so lucky that she isn't responsible for anything.

Abuela glares at my sister—well, at the back of my sister as she scoots out from under the bed. "You, young lady, need to be on your best behavior tonight."

Mirabel scrambles to her feet. Her eyes scan

the nursery in a way that doesn't look like someone who's going to be on her best behavior. Imagine if she interrupts dinner with the Guzmáns like she did with Antonio's party. Then Mariano won't propose, and then what will that mean for Bruno's vision? I'm supposed to live the life of my dreams!

"Sí, Mirabel," I say, trying to keep my voice light and airy. "I better not hear a sound out of you tonight."

Chapter 13 * Mirabel

MY AUNT AND UNCLE, my annoying cousins, my perfect sister, and my demanding grandmother hurry downstairs to welcome the Guzmáns. In the silence of the nursery, I slip in the last piece, one that had fallen on the floor. I stare at the puzzle, all the shards of Bruno's vision fitted together.

I can't believe what I'm seeing. I take off my glasses. I rub my eyes. Open them. Blink quickly several times. Put my glasses back on. Maybe I need more light. I go to the window and open the shutters wide. The late afternoon sun beams in, illuminating the vision.

It's me. Me and Casita. In a jigsaw image of emerald green shards, I can see a girl with wild hair, a big smile, and large glasses. Behind the girl in the image is a house, cracked and broken. This confirms it. I am part of the destruction of not only the house but also the magic. I take off my glasses again. The vision before me blurs.

"Who's ready for dinner with—?" Papá comes in the nursery and I jump. I try to cover the vision with my hands.

My father looks so worried. My face must be an open book—there's no way I can lie to him about why I'm upset. "Papá," I say. "I broke into Bruno's tower." My father gasps. I hurry with my story. I talk as quickly as possible. "And I found his last vision. Our family's in trouble. Luisa's gift is gone. Oh, Papá, the house will fall." I close my eyes and see Bruno's vision as clearly as if it were mine. "And I think it's all because of me!"

He looks down at the shards. "Mira," he says. He pulls the pieces apart and shoves them into his coat pocket.

"What are you—"

"We say nothing tonight." My father pats his pocket where the vision is hidden away like a secret. Another secret.

I love my papá, but I'm not so sure keeping secrets is the way to go here. "But—"

"Abuela wants tonight to be perfect. Your mother wants it to be perfect. So, until the Guzmáns leave, remember this: you did *not* break into Bruno's room. The family will *not* fall." Papá dusts off his hands and stands up, pulling me by my arms. The shards make a soft clanking noise in his jacket pocket. He grips me by both my shoulders and looks down into my eyes. "Just act normal."

Act normal? How am I supposed to do that? No one in this family is *ever* normal. But I suppose he has a point. Keep Abuela—and Isabela—happy. I clean my glasses with the edge of my blouse and put them back on. Now I can see my father clearly. He's so tall, I have to tilt my head a bit to look at him. He's in his best suit, the tie a little crooked. His mustache is neatly trimmed and his hair is combed back. His glasses have a smudge on one lens—probably some flour from Mamá. I love him so much. I reach up and give him the most Mirabel hug ever.

For a moment, we just stand there. Me and my dad, like two regular people who don't have an odd family, who aren't particularly special, but who love each other anyway.

"Dinner!"

Abuela's firm voice floats up the stairs and into my room, helped, no doubt, by Casita. The floorboards of the house gently shove us toward the door.

I reach up and try to smooth down my hair. Then I push my glasses up on my nose. I straighten my skirt—no time to fix that embroidery—and smooth out my blouse. I retie my shoes. I'm ready.

"No one will know," my father says.

As we turn to open the door, we see two blinking eyes across the courtyard. Dolores? Papá and I exchange glances. Of all the family members to be here. Chances are—with her hearing—she heard us and our secret. What will happen now?

Chapter 14 * Luisa

THE MADRIGAL CANDLE glows from the sideboard in the dining room, casting weird shadows on the walls and making the chandelier sparkle. The table—which I barely managed to wrestle into place—is set with the family's best china and silver for each of the thirteen guests: eleven Madrigals and two Guzmáns.

At first glance, everything looks pretty wonderful. But even with Mamá's cooking, Casita's beautiful dining room, and Abuela's determination, I'm not sure tonight's dinner is going to be as perfect as Abuela wants it to be.

When I slump into the empty chair beside Isabela, I notice how silent Mirabel is across the table. I know she's supposed to keep quiet tonight, but I'm learning that, lately, you should be prepared for anything. Camilo actually showed up as himself and is sitting beside Felix, and is chatting to Mariano across the table. Everyone seems to like Isabela's future fiancé. On the other side of the table is Dolores with her mother. Mamá is filling soup bowls with golden broth for the first course. My father is deep in conversation with Felix, as usual. I see that Abuela, at the head of the table, is keeping Mirabel at her side. On her other side is Doña Guzmán, who raises her glass.

"Doña Alma, we are honored to dine with la Familia Madrigal," says Doña Guzmán. Even when she smiles, Mariano's grandmother looks like she just tasted a sour guava. "Such a reputation! Although, when it comes to Mariano . . ." She gazes at her grandson with adoration. Her face softens. She must be a very different kind of grandmother than ours. Although we know Abuela loves us, she seems to have a hard time showing it. There have never been many cuddles from her. She always demands excellence from each of us. Now that my strength is . . . well, not quite as strong as it should be, I hope I can still perform for Abuela and make her proud. Tears come to my eyes when I think about my strength. I hope it comes back soon. "When it comes to Mariano," his grandmother repeats, "it's always best to see for myself."

Antonio pops up from under the table and grins. He's joined by three coatis who swing across the room.

Doña Guzmán looks a little startled to see animals at the table. Mariano laughs but stops when he sees his grandmother's glare. On the other hand, maybe it's just as hard to keep *her* happy.

"Yes, well," Abuela says, raising her own glass, "to a perfect night." Her eyes scan the table, boring into each family member's face as if she's daring anyone to misbehave. She pauses a long time on Mirabel, but Mirabel isn't paying attention. She and Dolores are staring at each other across the table. This is not good. What are they up to? I shake my head. As long as she keeps quiet, I suppose. That's all Abuela asked for.

"To a perfect night!" Abuela says, smiling. "¡Salud!"

"¡Salud!" all the guests repeat.

The abuelas share another toast, but they both exchange steely looks. Maybe Doña Guzmán isn't that different from Abuela; they both want what's best for their families.

"The entire Encanto was so relieved Antonio received his gift," Doña Guzmán says. I look down at my plate, trying to lift it with one finger like I used to do before—but it doesn't work. It takes my whole hand, and even then, it isn't effortless. What am I going to do? I try not to hyperventilate.

"Uh, yes," Abuela says with a smile that doesn't quite reach her eyes. Yikes. "Everyone, please eat. Buen provecho."

The tension eases as the food begins to make its way around the table. Dolores passes the potatoes and whispers something to Camilo. Her eyes bug out when his face turns into Doña Guzmán's! Not good. This is definitely not good. I knew something was not right. The potatoes—and the whispers—keep going around the table as Camilo turns to look right at me!

"Water?" Mariano asks.

Isabela, who doesn't seem to have noticed the whispers, nods demurely at her future fiancé. Her cheeks blush and match her dress. A few flower petals flit into her soup. That doesn't seem right, either.

Felix and Camilo are whispering. Felix seems

to choke and cough. A spray of half-chewed food flies across the table and lands on Doña Guzmán's plate. Abuela is going to be *so* mad!

"Ehem," she says. "Casita, a new plate for our guest."

But the house drops the new plate several times before finally setting one in front of Mariano's surprised grandmother. Doña Guzmán, though, is in a battle of politeness with Abuela. "It's nice to know that the magic is stronger than ever."

Double yikes. I can't help myself—I stifle a sob. Did she have to use that word? Strong? I can't even lift a puny little boulder!

"Yes, very, very true," Abuela says. "Mirabel? The salt?"

Mirabel fumbles with the saltshaker. "No problem, Abuela," she says with a weird grin on her face. "All I want to do is help this family."

Isabela glares at Mirabel.

Before Mirabel can respond, thunder crashes above Tía Pepa's head.

"Pepa!" Abuela shoots her a stern look. "The cloud, amor."

But it's too late. A small hurricane is forming above the beautifully laid table. If I still had my power, I would move the whole dining room somewhere drier. But I can't do anything. I start crying again. I can totally understand the storm cloud Pepa stirred up.

"Clear skies, clear skies," Pepa attempts. But the clouds stay. Now Mamá leans toward Pepa as if to comfort her. But then Pepa whispers something and Mamá's face goes pale. Nearly everyone's focus is now directed at either Mirabel or me. I try to keep my sobs under control.

And then, as if trying to prove she can get even weirder, Mirabel ducks her head under the table.

"Mirabel," Mariano calls, a teasing smile on his face. "Any more cracks?"

The whole family is quiet now, so everyone hears the conk Mirabel's head makes as she hits it on the way out from beneath the table.

"Or do you only see cracks when you're trying to get me and your sister off the dance floor?" he adds with a wink at me.

"Yes!" she says with a nervous giggle.

The family gasps.

"No, I mean, no. I just meant, yes, that's a very, uh, humorous question." Mirabel stands up. "And, um, speaking of questions—of *popping* questions. Was there anything you wanted to ask Isabela?"

I glance at Isabela. Her face is as red as the cloth on the table. Mamá is staring first at Isabela, then Mirabel, then Mariano. Doña Guzmán's hand flies to her chest in shock.

"Like," continues Mirabel, "right now?"

"Oh," the poor man says, "uh, I was actually gonna . . ."

"You were 'actually gonna.' Great," says Mirabel. What has gotten into her? Mirabel approaches Isabela, who looks like she might either faint or punch someone. Mirabel turns her to face Mariano.

"Since everyone here has a talent," Doña Guzmán says, not quite grasping what's going on . . . whatever it is, "my Mariano wanted to begin the night with a song." She looks around the table and her gaze lands on me. "Luisa! Could you bring the piano?"

My heart drops. I picture the heavy piano in the courtyard. I can feel some pesky tears stinging my eyes, threatening to burst. Just after, I get them under control. I really want to help, I do. I always like to help. But there's no way I can lift the piano right now! This is the worst night of my life!

"Luisa!" Isabela says, glaring at me. As if I'm stalling on purpose. I mean, I am stalling on purpose, but not for whatever purpose Isabela thinks.

"Ummm . . ." I say, frantically looking around. How am I going to get out of this without the Guzmáns figuring out that I've lost my gift?

"Actually," Mirabel says, "it's a family tradition to sing *after*."

Oh, I've never been so grateful for Mirabel in my whole life. I slink down the hallway and into the courtyard. Then I start pushing the piano toward the dining room door. Wow, is it ever heavy. No wonder everyone was so impressed with my strength. This is hard work. And boy, do the wooden legs on the tile floor make an awful screeching sound. What normally would have been effortless seems like it takes years. Everyone stares as I return to the dining room, flustered and out of breath.

Mariano seems to take this as his cue. He clears his throat, guffaws, and then turns to Isabela. She looks like if she could disappear into the eye of the hurricane that Tía Pepa is creating above us, she would. She glares at Mirabel as if everything is her fault.

"Isabela," he begins, "most graceful of all the Madrigals. The most perfect flower in this entire . . ."

He pauses. Isabela tries to smile sweetly at him,

but I can tell she's totally distracted by Mirabel, who's standing behind him, her almost fiancé, nodding like an out-of-control orchid in the breeze.

"The most perfect flower in this entire Encanto—"

A thunderclap booms from Pepa's storm. Things are getting worse.

Mirabel dances back and forth behind Mariano like she's trying to be a human shield to a moving target. She's making everyone dizzy. Then I see what she's hiding. Oh, dear. This is not good at all.

Cracks! Cracks in the Casa!

"Isabela, will you—"

Everything seems to happen in slow motion. Isabela's face goes from angelic to horrified as she, too, sees the cracks. Just above Mariano's head: cracks. The dining room walls are crisscrossed with cracks. Oh, geez! Cracks creep up the walls and invade the ceiling. The chandelier sways. Cracks head toward the door, toward the table where the

Madrigal candle burns. All the cracks are coming from where Mirabel is standing.

"What's happening?" Doña Guzmán cries.

The whole room freezes, even the cracks. We stare at one another. We know how badly Abuela wanted tonight to be perfect. And this—well, this is not perfect.

"Mirabel found Bruno's vision, and she's in it. She's going to destroy the magic and now we're all doomed!" Camilo blurts out in one giant breath.

Mariano looks at his grandmother, completely distracted from Isabela now. *My* grandmother is watching the cracks with one eye and keeping the other on Mirabel. Papá's face is pale and he grips my mother's hand. For once, Felix isn't laughing. Dolores looks like someone just gave her a poisoned mango. Antonio is trying to control his animals, but the coatis just clamber about. One jumps on me and then climbs over to Papá. Another coati reaches its little paws into Papá's coat pocket and pulls out something hard. Shards of green rattle as the coati assembles them on the dining table. Impressive animals.

It's Bruno's vision. And it has Mirabel's face on it. The whole family lurches in surprise, and at the same time, the Casa also lurches—although not from surprise. The cracks have worked their way around the room, and suddenly there's a *BOOM!* I jump out of the way just before the piano tips over with a crash. People fall out of their chairs, coatis fly through the air, and, for the finale, Pepa's storm cloud opens up.

Isabela's face goes from pale with shock to red with anger as she's drenched in icy cold rainwater. Her dress is soaked, and her hair drips into her face. I don't think I've ever seen her have a bad hair day, but this is definitely one. The flowers that were so perfect slide onto her lap. Her hands shoot up in surprise—and blue flowers and vines zing right into Mariano.

"My nose!" He clutches at his face. "She broke my nose!" he cries.

There is a thud, and all eyes swivel from Mariano's nose to the sideboard, where the candle tips over, dripping wax like an ice-cream cone. The candle, which usually stands so tall and straight and glows warm and golden, is mushed like a rotten banana. Next, we all turn to look at where Abuela's stare is fixed.

Mirabel stands there, frozen. "Abuela—" Our grandmother holds up her hand, but Mirabel continues. Or tries to. "I was going to tell you. . . . I wanted to help you. . . ."

The only sound in the dining room is Mariano groaning in pain.

Doña Guzmán pushes back her chair. "Come, Mariano!" she says.

Isabela doesn't move as her almost fiancé and his grandmother slink out of the dining room.

"Wait!" Abuela cries. "Please. Señora, por favor."

Doña Guzmán pauses. She turns. Oh, I do not like the look in her eyes. "This family is a disaster!"

she says and turns again, heading out the front door even as more cracks appear.

"Abuela, please," Mirabel says. If I were her, I'd be quiet right now.

"You," Abuela growls, pointing at Mirabel, "stay right there. Not another word. Go to your room!"

How is she supposed to stay there *and* go to her room? I would be so confused if I were her. But Mirabel doesn't seem to notice.

"It's not *my* fault!" she shouts.

We hear a screech, and everyone rushes out of the dining room. I'm just in time to see Doña Guzmán come face to face with a herd of tapirs. Where is Antonio? She shrieks and then yanks open the front door of la Casa.

"¡Felicidades!" the crowd waiting outside shouts as the band begins to play. Their smiles and the festive music slowly fade as they look at our faces.

The entire Madrigal family stares at the towns-people. They're clearly expecting a party. I guess news of the proposal traveled fast. I wonder how fast this *new* news will travel?

"I hate you!" Isabela shouts at Mirabel. Isa runs upstairs. Our mamá follows. This is too awful. I can't help bursting into tears myself. What will happen to us?

"Luisa—" Papá says, but I keep crying.

Crrrrack! Everyone turns and stares at Mirabel as more cracks thread their way through the house. If I still had my strength, I would hold the walls together. I reach out even though I know it won't help. Some habits are hard to break.

"You should have come to me," Mamá calls after Mirabel.

"I'm not doing this," Mirabel cries. "I'm not doing anything! It's not me, it's Bruno!"

"Bruno isn't here," Abuela booms.

A few gasps escape the crowd out front. The townspeople seem as if they want to leave the family to its own problems, and also like they want to stay because this is a really good show.

 148

"I know he's not," Mirabel says. But she seems distracted. I follow her gaze. I see a green glow and realize that it's a shard of the vision. The vision of her and the destruction of the Casa. And it's being carried by something . . . or someone.

Rats.

Not just one. Dozens of rats creep out of the cracks and scurry down the corridor. I look around to see if anyone else notices the rats hiding behind potted plants, scrambling over chairs, running under carpets. Mirabel's eyes behind her glasses get even bigger than usual. She stops protesting—and starts chasing them.

Abuela can't seem to decide which disaster to contend with first. She looks from the wandering animals to the crying family members to the townspeople. I see her falter for just a moment, like right before I'm about to lift something really heavy, like a church. I always pause, take a deep breath, remind myself I can do this, and then go. Abuela seems to be using the same trick. She straightens and grabs ahold of the big front door. "We are fine," she says in her rich, soothing voice. "The magic is strong!" she says, and shuts the door firmly. "We are the Madrigals!"

Isabela had wanted the evening of her proposal to be memorable. Well, we won't forget this disastrous night anytime soon.

Chapter 15 * Mirabel

RATS! I should have known. Thinking of the rats I spotted in Bruno's lair, I'm certain the rats must have something to do with him. Especially when they are carrying the shards from the vision! I have to find out where the rats are going. I have to prove to my family that I didn't do anything wrong. Or, at least, I don't think I did. I have to figure out what Bruno has to do with all the cracks, the tipped-over candle, the disastrous evening. It *can't* all be my fault.

"Lo siento," I whisper, mostly to myself. "I'm sorry, Abuela."

I run after the trail of rats as they pitter-patter up the stairs and along the balcony, glowing green shards in their teeth. Pepa's thunderstorm has expanded from the dining room to the whole house. Thunderclaps shake the foundation. Lightning flashes. And in that spark of light, I spot a rat disappearing under a large painting, one I've walked past a million times without really seeing it.

I pull at the heavy frame, revealing a dusty wall—and an opening. It's a secret passageway! I check over my shoulder for Abuela or Isabela. No one is around. No humans, anyway. Another rat scurries through the opening. This time I follow.

My eyes blink in the blackness. Slowly, they adjust to the dark. The narrow passageway goes to the left and the right. Pinpricks of light poke through at various intervals, and I realize these are nail holes and light fixtures. I'm behind the walls of Casita. I'm *in* the walls.

I start walking and the pinpricks increase. Now the light is not just from nail holes; it's coming through the cracks. The farther I walk, following the rats, the more light and the more cracks I see. Even in the near darkness, I can see the rats with the shards of the vision, the green glow illuminating their path and mine.

What if the cracks *are* my fault? I think of Isabela's devastated face, Abuela's look of horror. If I'm part of Bruno's vision, does that mean I'm causing the destruction? I stop walking. Maybe if I'm very still, the house will stop breaking.

I stand for what feels like a century, not moving a muscle. The only sounds are the scurrying of rat feet, the pounding rain from Pepa's storm, and my own heavy breathing. As I stand there like a statue, my eyes follow the trail of the green glow. The glow moves into the air. Can the rats fly?

And then: a bolt of lightning.

There in front of me, illuminated for a moment, is a figure. The tall frame is hunched under a wool poncho. The bony hands clutch at its folds as if readying themselves to lunge at me. At the next flash of lightning, his eyes meet mine. They are dark, almost black, and empty-looking. His face is pale and his mouth a sharp grimace. I feel a shiver run down my spine. I force myself not to squeeze my eyes shut. I need to find out more. He holds the rat in his hand and takes the shard. And then he's gone.

Bruno! My uncle is the key to unlocking the mystery of the vision. He doesn't look like some-one who wants company (or like someone I really want to hang out with), but I need to ask him so many questions. *Why am I part of his vision? What*

happened to him? Why is the house falling apart? What's with the rats?

"Stop!" I yell.

He freezes for a split second and then bolts away.

I start running after him.

The passageway between the walls is narrow and uneven. I focus on not tripping and not losing him. The only sound is the pounding of our feet. In the dim light, I catch sight of him every so often, and then he disappears again. Into a shadow, around a corner, through a crack. Old trusses crisscross the walls, and broken floorboards poke up here and there. When I lose sight of him, I just keep going. The passageway appears to be a one-way-only kind of place, so I don't need to see in order to know that I'm headed in the right direction.

I listen to the beat of his feet on the boards. Every once in a while, my foot slips through a crack in the floor and I have to scramble up again.

"Stop!" I call. "Bruno!" The walls echo, "Bru . . . Bru . . . Bru . . . no . . . no . . . no . . ."

He doesn't stop. We run up and down. Twists and turns catch me. I trip. Fall more than once. I smash into a wall when I take the turn too tightly. *Ouch*, that hurt. A cloud of plaster dust makes me sneeze. I get up, though, and keep going, keep following Bruno, the only one who might be able to unravel this mystery.

And then, up ahead, I see him in another flash of lightning. He leaps across a chasm of black nothingness. I'm afraid he's getting away. Along with all the answers.

I skid to a stop. I peer into the void below. Can I make it across the chasm? Bruno did, but he's tall and probably pretty used to jumping over chasms. I'm just a kid. This is not an area of expertise for me. I can hear Bruno's steps fading. I have to try if I'm going to catch up with him. I take a deep breath, fortifying my courage with thoughts of my family and my Casita. And then I leap . . .

"No!"

I'm falling.

"Help! ¡Ayúdame, Casita!" I catch hold of something hard and cold. But my grip isn't firm enough. Below me is the black nothingness. My feet dangle. I concentrate on my fingers and their grip. I can do this. I think? If only I were as strong as Luisa. My fingers slip. "Help me!"

My mind races. I always try so hard to do the right thing, but somehow, I always manage to get it wrong. I only wanted to reach Bruno so that he could tell me what his vision was. And now I'll never find out. Isabela is right—I *do* ruin everything. Now what will happen to the house? The family? What will Mamá and Papá say when they realize I'm gone for good?

One minute I'm flailing in thin air, the next I feel a strong hand on mine. I'm being grabbed by an unseen savior. The arm hoisting me up is skinny and willowy, but strong enough to hold me. I think I might be crying with relief. It's not over yet!

I look up to see who my rescuer is. In the light through the cracks, I see a scrawny, timid figure. He's swimming in a huge woolen poncho three sizes too big. He's unshaven and haggard. It's Bruno! I open my mouth to scream. Then I study his face. He looks frightened—petrified—maybe even more so than I am. His eyes aren't wild—they're sad. His face is creased with frown lines as if he's been sad for many, many years.

He's pulling me to safety, but my hand is slipping.

"You're very—ergh!—sweaty," he says.

It's true that my palms sweat when I'm worried. Isabela is always telling me not to touch her things because my hands are too grubby. And I'm definitely anxious right now, what with almost falling in a chasm. I feel a nervous laugh bubbling up. But then the floorboards on which he's standing give way. He hurls me to safety but loses his own footing. I watch in horror as another blast of lightning reveals my tío Bruno falling to his death.

I brace for the fading cry for help, the final terrified scream.

But all I hear is a thud.

"Ouch," he says in a rough voice from not very far away. "Huh."

I peer over the edge of the chasm. It isn't a chasm at all. Just a hole in the floor. A big hole, but still, just a hole. Bruno is brushing himself off. With one big step he's out of the not-chasm chasm.

"Um," he says. He looks at me. Looks down. He pulls his hood further over his head. Looks into the far-off distance. "Bye."

And he walks away.

At first, I'm too stunned to move. Then I cry, "What? Wait!"

Not again. Ah, geez!

It's time to chase my uncle. *Again.*

I follow him through the back of the house, the inside, between rooms and behind stairs. I wonder what Casita thinks of all this roaming around. Bruno fumbles forward. I can tell where in the house we are by the sounds and smells on the other side of the walls. I hear a sobbing Luisa. I hear the squeaks of the chigüiros in Antonio's room. I hear the clatter of dishes in the dining room. I keep running. I'm gaining on him because Bruno steps around the cracks in the floor. Each time he passes a beam of wood, he knocks on it—almost as if he's superstitious. I realize he's not really trying to get away from me. He's heading somewhere. *Where is he going?*

"Why was I in your vision, Tío?" I call, trying to keep pace with his quick walking and his starts and stops. "What does it mean? Is it why you came back?"

He stops again and I almost bump into him. "Uno, dos, tres, four," he says, rapping on the wall. "Five, six."

"Uh? Bruno?"

"You were never supposed to see that vision. No one was—a little salt." He walks a few paces and then tosses salt over his shoulder before stuffing the shaker back in his pocket.

I sneeze. "What do you mean?"

"My three whistles," he says and puts his lips together. Then he spins around. I've got to say this: he seems quite loco. "There, that's better," he says, and keeps walking.

As I follow him deeper—or higher—or both?—into the house, I notice that the cracks on this side of the wall have been fixed. Well, sort of. It isn't very neat or well done.

"Have you been patching the cracks?" I ask.

He pauses and looks at the dried material that covers the cracks as if he's never seen it before. "Oh, no," he says. "I'm too scared to go near those cracks. All the patching is done by Hernando."

There are *more* people living in the walls? What the heck is going on? "Who's Hernando?"

Bruno pulls the hood of his poncho over his head. "I'm Hernando," he says in a low voice. "I'm not scared of nothing."

I stare at him. He is *not* doing well. This is the guy that's supposed to save me, the house, and the magic? I'm starting to think this might not be the best plan. On the other hand, I have no other plan.

Then he smiles briefly and pulls back the hood. "Actually, it's me." Then he adds, in a squeaky voice, "I'm Jorge. I make the Spackle."

"Huh." I stare at my uncle. Is this why no one talks about Bruno? "So, uh, how long have you been back?"

Instead of answering, though, Bruno keeps going. And as I follow him, I realize that he's been living in these tunnels for a long time. Then he takes another turn and there's a door. Not a glowing, magic door. Just an ordinary door. A plain, beat-up, ancient-looking door on crooked hinges.

It opens with a creak. I follow him inside. His room. A real, lived-in room. Small, dark. Makes my nursery room look like luxury. There is evidence of a life lived, however oddly, in every corner. Blankets and broken lamps, chipped teacups and moth-eaten sweaters, loose screws and coiled piano strings.

A thought dawns on me. I have always imagined Bruno living in some faraway place, not wanting any reminders of the family he left behind so mysteriously. But this is the room of someone who wishes he were with his family.

"You never left, did you?"

I think of my own nursery, decorated with my own bits of treasures and drawings. Personalized to make it feel more like mine. Am I as crazy as my tío?

"Well," Bruno says, "I left my tower, which was, you know, a lot of stairs."

Uh-huh, I think. *Because of the stairs. Sure.*

"And in here, I'm kitchen adjacent." He grins. I

hear the clanging of pots and pans and the smell of Mamá's cooking on the other side of the wall. He paces from the table to the corner. "Plus, free entertainment!"

I follow his gaze to a cardboard puppet theater. Only, clearly, it's not for puppets. It says RAT THEATER in messy, dripping ink.

"What kind of entertainment do you like?" he asks. "Sports? Thrillers? Telenovelas?" Bruno takes two of his rats and sets them on the makeshift stage. "Look," he says, "their love could never be."

I stare at the rats, the theater, Bruno.

"I don't understand," I say at last. Why is Bruno living in the walls? Why is he hiding from the Familia Madrigal? Does it have anything to do with the crumbling Casa?

"Well, because she's his aunt and she has amnesia. So she can't remember that she's his aunt. See what I said? It's like a very forbidden kind of—"

I pull Bruno away from his rat theater.

"No, I don't understand why you left." I think of his tower that overlooks the Casa. And I think of this space behind the walls, still looking over the Casa. "But didn't leave."

He looks down like he's a little boy in trouble at school. "You see, because the mountains around the Encanto are pretty tall." He shifts his weight from one foot to the other. "And, like I said, I have free food and everything." He picks up a plate from a table. The table has drawings on it so it looks as if he were sitting with the familia. There's a sketch of a place setting for Abuela and Mamá and Pepa. More for me and my sisters and my cousins. And his own. He's been trying to make himself feel not quite so alone with this make-believe dining table. My heart thrums in sympathy. I know what it's like to feel lonely.

"My gift, uh, wasn't helping the family," he says sadly. "But I love my family, ¿sabes? I just don't know how to, um, you know. . . ."

He looks at me and, for a moment, I can see his eyes clearly. He loves his family, just like me. And just like me, I realize, he wasn't helping them.

"Anyway, I think you should go, because—well, I don't have a good reason." He slumps in a lumpy chair. "But I'm getting really uncomfortable, so I think you should go."

I put my hand on his arm to try to calm him. That's what I did for Antonio when he used to have nightmares in the nursery. I would sit on the edge of his bed in the dark and rest my hand on his little body. Sometimes we just need to feel that another human is there.

"Why was I in your vision?" I ask softly. "What does it mean?" Bruno doesn't answer. I take a deep breath. "My whole life I just wanted to make the family proud of me for once. But if I should stop— if I'm hurting our family—I just need to know. Please tell me."

Bruno is silent. But I can feel him relaxing under my hand, just like Antonio would.

I wait. He'll tell me when he's ready. A little bit of patience can go a long way.

"I can't tell you."

Great. I sigh. This is not going well.

"Because I don't know."

I look up at him. He plays with the shards, moves them around. They make quiet clinking noises as they bump into each other. He fumbles with them until they create the vision. The image I saw in my room.

"I had this vision the night you didn't get your gift," he begins. "Abuela never thought I saw anything good, but she was worried about the magic, and she begged me to look into the future, to see what it meant. So I did."

He shifts uncomfortably. I think about how it's hard to not do what Abuela asks, even if you know it might not be a good idea.

"I saw our house in danger. Breaking. The magic in danger. And then I saw you. But the vision was different; what you'd see changed. No one answer.

No fate." Bruno's forehead wrinkles. "But I knew how it was going to look to everyone when I told them what I saw." Bruno stares into my eyes, pleading. "I knew how it was going to look because I'm Bruno and everyone assumes the worst."

I stare at him. I think about how everyone assumes that I'm going to screw up everything I do. I see Isabela watching me, just waiting for me to wipe my nose on my sleeve or get my skirt caught in my underwear. I know Mamá is always ready to cure me with an arepa because she expects me to skin my knee or cut my hand. I know Abuela keeps an eye out for me, knowing that, without a gift, I can't make the family proud like the others can.

"So, yeah, I destroyed the vision. I don't know how things will go. But my guess? Whatever is happening—the cracks, the magic—the fate of our entire family—it's going to come down to you."

"Me?"

The fate of the family comes down to *me*? My uncle and I—the two forgotten and misunderstood members of the Madrigal family—don't move. My head spins and I close my eyes. I'm the only Madrigal without a gift, without magic. I'm the one person in the family who doesn't quite belong. How can the fate of the Madrigals depend on *me*? Abuela is the head of the family, so she should be able to figure this out. Or Mamá with her power to heal. Or maybe Luisa could fix everything with her strength. Isabela might calm the cracks with flowers, or Dolores might be able to hear the Casa say what's wrong. Even jokester Camilo would be better at determining the fate of the family than I ever could be.

I can hear the noises the Casa makes, the sounds that must be so familiar to Bruno: creaks and groans, clatters and clanks. It's hard to believe that this messy inside is part of the beautiful outside, all of it making up what is my beloved Casita.

"But," Bruno says, breaking the silence between us, "you dug up the vision and showed the family. So who knows? Maybe you *do* wreck everything."

If I were in my room right now, I would hide my head under my covers and never get up. Bruno grabs a coffee cup from a table and brings it to his lips absently. Then he stops, fishes out a bedraggled rat, and takes a sip. Ew.

"Or you don't. It's a mystery," he continues, his voice a little breathless and crazed again. "I mean, that's what my visions are. Look, if I could help you any more, I would. But, um, that's all I saw. What's next is up to you."

And with that, he opens the door to his little room and ushers me toward it with fake chivalry, as if he were a gentleman instead of a weird uncle living inside the walls.

Chapter 16 * Mirabel

STANDING IN THE DIM LIGHT behind the walls, I hear a voice. It sounds like it's just a few inches away.

"It was supposed to be perfect!"

It sounds like it might be Isabela.

The voice's owner continues, "I hate her!"

Yep, definitely my oldest sister.

"Oye," I hear Mamá say, "Luisa's gift is completely gone!"

I shift my feet. The sand on the ground between the walls is gritty beneath my shoes.

"How do we even know the Encanto is still safe?" It's the anxious voice of my uncle Felix. He never worries about anything.

"Is she going to make me lose *my* magic?" Camilo's voice has no hint of humor. It's hard for me to imagine my cousin being this serious.

"Everything," someone says in a firm voice, "everything we've built is at stake!" It feels like my grandmother is at my side as she says this. I picture her, inches away, on the other side of the wall. Inside the house. On the right side of the walls. "Open your eyes!" she says. "Mirabel was in that vision for a reason."

The voices of all my family members clash and smash in my head. *Safe? Completely gone! I hate her! For a reason . . .*

A green glow seeps out from under Bruno's door. I picture him hiding inside, far from the family, alone with his rats, uncooperative. That's no way to be: hidden away inside the walls, here but not here. I pound on the door and then push it open. I have an idea.

"What if you have another vision?" I demand.

Bruno looks terrified. I didn't mean to scare him.

"What?" Bruno shrinks into his poncho. "Oh, no," he says. "No, no, no, no." Bruno holds up his hands and shakes his head vigorously. "I don't do visions anymore. Nope."

"But you could. . . ." I step toward him and he stumbles back. "You can't tell me the weight of the world is on my shoulders . . . *the end*. If our family's fate is up to me," I say, "then 'me' says, have another vision. Maybe it'll show me what to do."

"That's a bad idea."

"It's a great idea." I paste a cheery smile on my face.

"Look, even if I wanted to—which I don't—you wrecked my vision cave." My eyes dart away from his. Oops. "Yeah, I know about that."

I picture Bruno's massive cave, the steps, the weird sculpture, the sand avalanche. I wouldn't think anyone would miss that place. But I do feel bad for destroying it.

"And that's a problem because I need a big open space."

"We'll figure it out." I grab his hand and pull him toward the door. "Come on. The two family weirdos, finding each other? It's meant to be."

Bruno harrumphs. "I still need a big open space."

Croak!

Bruno and I both jump at the sight of Antonio's toucan. Where does this thing come from? We turn and suddenly there are a couple of tapirs, several lumbering chigüiros, and a jaguar. Oh, and there's Antonio.

Antonio!

"They told me everything," my primito says. As

if that explains what he's doing here with all his animal friends. They snuffle and waddle around the room, digging into piles of dirty laundry and sticking their noses into broken jugs. The animals make Bruno's room look even smaller and sadder.

Bruno stares at the jaguar, which is eyeing his rats hungrily.

Antonio looks down at his jaguar. "Don't eat those."

I reach out and ruffle Antonio's hair. I'm so glad he's here. Who would have guessed that his gift—communicating with animals—could be so useful? Then I turn to Bruno. "Our family is in trouble. We can help them."

He avoids my eyes.

I wait until he looks at me. "You deserve to come home."

Bruno stands in the middle of Antonio's rain forest room looking a little uneasy. It's not clear what he thinks of the jungle. A crowd of coatis gathers to watch whatever is about to happen. A chigüiro sniffs the ground and then looks at Bruno expectantly. The toucan croaks a couple times, but when Antonio shushes it, the croaking stops.

"We need to hurry," I say as the room shakes, reminding us of the trouble the Casa is in.

"You can't hurry the future," Bruno says. "Everything's got to be perfect."

Ugh! He sounds like Abuela. Why does everything always have to be perfect?

"Um . . ." Bruno says, looking at Antonio, whose new friend, the jaguar with deep black spots, sits beside my uncle, licking its lips. "Is that thing going to eat me?"

Antonio and the jaguar look at one another. The jaguar chuffs. Antonio turns back to Bruno and shrugs. "Not today." But the way he says it makes it seem as if the matter will be open for discussion tomorrow.

Bruno crosses himself. He sure is superstitious.

"The rats told me you don't wash your underwear."

"Antonio!" I cry. "That was rude!"

"It's true," Antonio says with a giggle.

Bruno's face turns from pale to embarrassed red. "You have a wonderful gift, Antonio," he says with a gulp. The ground shakes again, and the coatis look up with startled eyes.

Bruno shakes himself like a boxer preparing for a fight. He takes a handful of sand and starts making a large circle. The tapirs stand at the circle's edge, their toes inches from the line of sand. Antonio's chigüiro ambles in without a care in the world and sits right in the circle's path. Bruno detours the circle around it. Macaws caw from above us.

Bruno looks up at me. "What if I can't do it?"

I reach out but don't touch him. "You can, Tío."

"What if I show you something worse?" he asks, looking down at the sand. "If I see something bad, it'll happen. Won't it?"

"I don't think you make bad things happen,"

I reassure him. If he gets worked up again, he'll never show me his vision. "I just think most people can only see things in a certain way."

Antonio nods. He stands beside Bruno, holding the little stuffed jaguar I made him. My heart squeezes. I'm so proud that, even though Antonio has real animal friends now, he still loves the pretend one I gave him. "Here," Antonio whispers. "For good luck. For the nerves." He shoves the stuffed animal at Bruno. "But, um, I'm gonna need that back, okay?"

Bruno looks at the stuffed animal, then at Antonio, then at me.

"You can do this," I whisper.

From the folds of his poncho, Bruno pulls out a case, some ancient-looking gold container. The gold is decorated with symbols and designs. He snaps it open and takes out a match. When he strikes the match, Antonio's jungle flashes. Then Bruno ignites a few damp leaves at four different points around the circle. They begin to smolder.

"I can do this. I can do this. I can do this," he repeats.

His mantra isn't giving me a lot of confidence. Isn't seeing the future his gift? Shouldn't he be a little less nervous about using it?

Bruno starts to count, over and over. "Uno, dos, tres, four, five, six. Uno, dos, tres . . ." The smudgy smoke begins to curl into the air. It spirals around the circle. Around and around. "Uno, dos, tres, four, five, six," he repeats.

Magic fills Antonio's room. It swirls around us. The waterfalls splash and the leaves on the palms sway. The circling breeze blows my hair in my face. Sparkly light glitters like thousands of luciér-nagas flitting through the air. The circle around Bruno glows brighter. I'm not sure if I should be scared—or amazed.

"You might want to hang on." Bruno reaches out and takes my hand, gripping it tightly.

I'm not scared at all now. *Really.*

Pretty soon Bruno's vision flashes around us. I

can see what he's seeing—colors, lights, shapes. Wind roars in my ears. There's the Casa and the cracks. There's Abuela. The Casa again. The cracks. I see myself standing in the epicenter of everything.

"I can't!" Bruno cries as if he is in pain, dropping my hand. He pulls away, looking as if he could hide himself in the folds of his poncho. "I have to stop!"

"No!" I shout, taking his hands in mine once more. He can't stop now. We have to see the whole vision. No matter what it shows. You can never be sure of anything if you don't get the whole picture.

Bruno shakes his head sadly like he's about to give up. I think of his sad little room. He has a lot of practice with giving up. He just needs someone to believe in him. A rumble grumbles under our feet. The Casa must be shifting again, the magic sifting away like sand. The trees in Antonio's room tremble and sway. He can't stop now!

"There's got to be more," I cry. "Something we're not seeing!"

"There's nothing else."

"Tío Bruno," I say in a whisper. "The family needs you."

And then something catches my eye. The vision swirling around us slows, and I spot a butterfly. A small blue butterfly with iridescent wings, the kind Antonio likes to catch (and release) on warm days in the Encanto. My eyes follow the flitting wings as it glides toward a glowing light. "There! Over there!"

"The butterfly," Bruno says. "Follow the butterfly. . . ." It's almost as if he's in a trance. He mumbles. The butterfly flutters, its wings blue then gold, shining and sparkling. "Someone else," he says. "There's someone else."

"Who?" I try to see what he's seeing. But I don't have his gift.

"Embrace her . . ." he says in a monotone.

The butterfly is closer to the golden glow, and out of the glow, the shape of a woman appears. I can't tell who it is. Is it Abuela? Is it me?

". . . you will see the way."

"Who is it, Bruno?"

"Embrace her," Bruno repeats.

I squint, trying to make out the figure as it gets closer. Bruno just keeps telling me to embrace her, that I will see the way. But I don't see anything!

"*Who* is it?" I shout.

And then I see who it is.

Isabela.

"Embrace her. You will see the way."

"Are you kidding me?" I cry. "Me? Embrace Isabela?"

My voice echoes as the vision extinguishes itself.

"Your sister!" He snaps out of his vision trance. "That's great!"

I stare at Bruno. How can he think that's great? We need to get moving. I grab his hand and pull him out of Antonio's room. The animals watch us go in complete confusion. "Embrace Isabela! What does that even mean? Is that a hug?"

Out on the balcony, no one is around. I look into the courtyard below, but it's empty, too, luckily. My sister! I snort. Embrace her? I want to laugh.

I drag Bruno toward Isabela's door. The walls of the corridor are crisscrossed with thin cracks. Outside her room, we don't knock. Instead, we hide—I mean, like, just hang out—behind a couple of potted plants. Bruno and I peer between the big leaves at Isabela's perfect door. Flowers. Pink. Lavender. That nice little glow all the magic rooms get. Humph!

"Why would a hug make me 'see the way'?" I hiss. "She won't hug me. She hates me. Also, I ruined her proposal—"

"Mirabel," Bruno begins.

"It's just annoying. Of course it's Isabela." I shake my head. "Señorita Perfecta always has to have all the answers—"

"Mirabel," Bruno says again. "Sorry, um, you're missing the point." I shoot him one of those if-looks-could-kill kind of glares. "The fate of the family is not up to her. It's up to *you*. And before you say you can't get a hug . . . you helped Antonio get his door, you helped me have my first good vision ever, you've never given up once." I stare at Bruno. Is this really what he thinks? "You're the best of us. You just have to see it."

The best? I can't believe what I'm hearing. I wouldn't mind embracing *him* right now. Maybe that would do something?

"By yourself." Bruno studies his dirty finger-nails. "After I leave."

"Wait, what?" I say. "You're not coming?"

I stare in disbelief as Bruno scoots himself and the plant backward toward the painting—the one with the secret passageway. "It was *your* vision, not mine."

I take it back about that hug. I fold my arms

over my chest. I see what's going on here. "You're afraid Abuela will see you."

Bruno pulls at the picture frame. "Yep, I mean, yes. That, too." He ducks through the opening. "If you save the magic, uh . . . come visit."

"*When* I save the magic," I say with a grin, "I'm bringing *you* home."

Bruno disappears into the wall, mumbling to his rats. With Bruno gone, I feel very alone. The house is eerily quiet. I turn around and look across the courtyard at the candle in Abuela's window. The flame is flickering unevenly, and the light is even dimmer. Wax pools around its base. It doesn't matter if I feel alone or if I'm not sure I can do this. I have to try.

"You're going to be okay, Casita," I say with a sigh. I lay my hand against Casita's cool plaster. I stand up straight and walk to Isabela's door. I whisper to myself, "Just gonna save the magic. And the family."

Chapter 17 * Isabela

"YOU SHOULD HAVE told me the moment you saw it, Agustín," Abuela scolds Papá in front of the rest of the Madrigals, and I know she is talking about Bruno's vision that Mirabel found. "Think of the family!"

"She's my daughter," he says. The way he says the word "daughter" digs into my heart. After all I do to try to be perfect, I can't help wondering if

Mirabel is still his favorite. Maybe I need to try harder. I want to make everything okay, but I know that flowers won't help right now. I bite my lip and stay quiet. "Does she not count?" Papá demands.

Abuela is about to protest when Felix bursts in. Wait, that's not Felix.

"Abuela!" shouts the fake Felix, who shifts into Camilo. "The town wants you. They're freaking out!"

"Camilo!" the real Felix scolds. He looks ready to box Camilo's ears.

My father might be off the hook, I think as Abuela scans the faces of the family. But she seems to be looking for something. Or someone. Here comes more drama. "Where is she?" Abuela asks. No one answers. "Where is Mirabel?"

I look around, but she's not with us. Neither is Antonio, I realize. My primito must be enjoying his new rain forest room and his animal friends. Oh, to be young and carefree and not have to think about marriage proposals or dying magic.

He's lucky he doesn't have to worry about Mirabel ruining his life.

Abuela follows Camilo outside. I turn the other way and escape to my room, where at least I can have a moment of peace.

After I close my door, I feel much better. The soft light of my room is soothing, and so is the gentle tinkle of the lily pads floating lazily in the pond. Fireflies flit from branch to branch. The mirror at my dressing table reflects the cool blue glow of the lanterns. The smell of dahlias greets me. Their pretty flower faces look at me with serene calm. I take a deep breath. In. Out. It takes practice to be as calm as I appear. In. Out. I notice that the azalea next to my bed has a fading blossom. I snap it off. I don't like to have anything out of order. In. Out.

I'm about to collapse on my bed—in fact, I've already removed my shoes and lined them up carefully—when there's a banging on the door.

"Isabela!"

I groan. Mirabel. Why is she at *my* door? She makes me so mad. Usually, I can keep so calm and collected. But around Mirabel, I get irritated. I picture her standing at my pretty floral door knocking. I just want her to go away. I'm inspired to do this cool trick I don't use very often. Through the door, I can hear her gasp of surprise as the doormat's bouquet of flowers rearranges itself from WELCOME to GO AWAY. I really don't have time—or patience—for Mirabel right now.

"Isa, I know we've had our issues," she says through the door. "But I'm . . . ready to be a better sister. Because you've always been such a . . . perfect sister to me." Her voice snags like she doesn't really believe what she's saying. And neither do I.

Now the doormat says I DON'T CARE.

"So, we should just, um, hug it out," she says with false cheer.

"Hug it out?" I shout. "Luisa can't lift an empanada; Mariano's nose looks like a smashed papaya."

I hear a creak. Mirabel has the nerve to actually enter my room! How dare she!

"Isa," she says, "I know you're upset. And you know what cures being upset?" She comes closer.

I perch on the edge of my neatly made bed, ignoring my sister. My fingers trace the pattern of the lacy coverlet. Maybe she'll leave if I don't answer.

"A warm embrace." She smiles as if that is going to make everything better.

"Get out."

Instead of getting out, she comes even closer. Her hands and face are dirty; her hair is even more of a mess than usual. What has she been doing? She looks like she's been digging in a sandbox. "Isa—"

I stand, inching away from her. What has gotten into her? She opens her arms. As if I would embrace her!

"Everything was perfect!" I shout. I've had

enough! "Abuela was happy. The family was happy. You want to make things better? Apologize for ruining my life!"

Mirabel opens her mouth to protest, but I make a vine pop out and stop her. A flower covers her mouth. She spits out the petals.

"Okay, okay," she mumbles. "I am sorry," she begins, "that your life is so great!"

That's it! She doesn't even know how to apologize. She can't do anything right! "Out!" I yell at her.

I wave my hands and more vines sprout, wrapping around Mirabel's feet. I really don't like to use my gift in this way, but Mirabel has pushed me to the end of my patience.

"Go! Goodbye!" My vines drag her toward the door, but Mirabel grabs the leg of my desk.

"Wait! Isabela, fine. I apologize. I wasn't trying to ruin your life." She grips the chair with both hands as the vine pulls more tightly. "Some of us have bigger problems, you stupid, selfish, entitled princess!"

I gasp. "Selfish!" The flowers at my feet turn scarlet, as red as blood. I can feel my hands tense and my jaw tighten. "I've been stuck being perfect my entire life. The only thing you've ever done for me is mess things up—"

"Nothing is messed up! You can still marry that big dumb hunk and—"

"I never wanted to marry Mariano!" I shout. I can't believe I just said that out loud. The red flowers deepen. Their petals sharpen. And there, between me and my sister, a cactus grows, its spines as angry and menacing as I feel. "I was doing it for the family!"

"Isa . . ." Mirabel stares at the cactus, then me. "You don't want to marry him?"

"No!" I shout. "And I don't want to be perfect all the time. Look at this!" I point at the cactus. I get a little too close to a spine, which pricks my finger. A drop of blood appears. "I don't want to always have to create beautiful, boring flowers. What about what I want? What if I want something ugly? What if I want something different?"

"Uh." Mirabel backs up a bit. "The cactus is pretty, actually," she says. "It's just pretty in a different way."

I pant. Slowly, my breathing calms. I turn back toward the cactus and look at it again. What do you know? Mirabel is right. "Yeah, it is, isn't it?" I point my fingers at the cactus. It grows taller. It sprouts red blobs—are those blossoms? "Pretty in an ugly way?" I keep going, pointing my hand around my room. My headboard sprouts gray-green vines covered in little black nubs.

"Pretty ugly?" Mirabel says with a grin.

Brown moss inches across the floor, heading toward my desk. A strange tree with a twisted trunk winds itself around my wardrobe. Sage-colored lichen becomes a bumpy tablecloth. Leaves from the Tabebuia tree turn yellow and flutter down.

"Pretty, no?" I say as more cacti sprout, twisting and turning until they're tall as trees. "Is this perfect?"

"It's perfectly you, Isabela," Mirabel says. "How about a hug?"

But I'm just getting started. A jacaranda shoots up, followed by strangling figs that land over the sea of moss. I think about how Mirabel lives, how she decorates her room with her own designs, how she wanders from room to room, from family member to family member, never caring what anyone thinks of her, never trying to be perfect. Just being herself. "What if I grew plants that I wanted to grow? What if I didn't worry about them being beautiful—whatever that means?"

"Do it, Isabela!" she shouts.

"I think I will." I wave my arms and my plants grow. Beautiful, colorful. Ugly, unique. Twisty, viny, spiny. All of them growing together in a big, wonderful tangle of me-ness. They glow in the golden light of—the Madrigal candle? Mirabel and

I stare out my door as the candle burns brighter.

"There's nothing you can't do, hermana." Mirabel grins at me. Like she really sees me, like she's proud to be my sister, even if what I'm doing right now is definitely not perfect.

We whoop and run through the greenery, laughing like small children. I haven't felt this free or this happy since . . . well, since ever, maybe.

I keep growing weirder and weirder plants, Mirabel cheering me on. We run out to the balcony, the delicate flowers from Antonio's gift day replaced with weird green vines. We dance the cumbia and then a waltz through the flowers and the vines. We laugh and laugh—until we find ourselves crashing over the railing of the balcony and into the courtyard below. Luckily, our fall is cushioned by the piles of leaves and vegetation at our feet. Mirabel and I are dazed but unhurt. I reach out to embrace her—

"What have you done?"

We freeze.

"Abuela?" Mirabel squeaks.

What have I done? I look around at the mess. Papá and Mamá follow Abuela. Suddenly the beautifully ugly and ugly-beautiful plants look like a disaster, not a wonderful creation. I've disappointed my family. I shouldn't have listened to Mirabel. I'm supposed to help the family—not make a mess!

Chapter 18 * Luisa

WHENEVER THERE'S a crash around here, it usually means my help is needed. So when I hear a loud crash from the courtyard, I stop staring at the wheelbarrow of bricks I want nothing more than to have the strength to pick up in the front yard and run inside Casita.

"Abuela, it's okay. Everything is going to be okay," Mirabel is babbling as I enter the courtyard.

I take a step forward and stop. Mirabel is sitting in a pile of vegetation that looks like maybe it used to be pretty flowers. Abuela stands in the middle of a giant mess with our parents close behind her. Unless they want me to help move this pile of rubbish, the scene doesn't look like something I could fix even *if* I hadn't lost my gift.

"Okay?" Abuela repeats. "Look around! Look at your sister!"

That's when I realize there's someone else in the middle of the mess. I blink. My eyes must be fooling me. Maybe I was in the sun for too long. Isabela—*Isabela?!*—is also in the heap of plants and vines, looking just as disheveled as our sister. Their faces are streaked with dirt. Isabela's dress is crisscrossed with green stains, and she has wilted petals and dried leaves in her hair.

"Look at our home," Abuela says.

Obediently, I look around the house. In addition to the mess in the courtyard, there are even more cracks in the walls than before. Something strange and black grows along the railing of the balcony. The bricks in the courtyard are uneven, and bits of plaster dust the floorboards. The portraits of my family are skewed at various angles. Maybe if I just straightened that picture of Abuelo . . . I touch the frame with my pinkie finger. It barely moves. I try again, this time with more *oomph.* Oops. It tumbles off the wall, leaving more cracks.

"If you just . . ." Mirabel says, pushing her crooked glasses up on her nose. She takes a deep breath and begins again. "Isabela wasn't happy—"

"Of course she wasn't happy!" Abuela says angrily. I back up into the shadows a bit. Just because I'm strong—I used to be strong (don't cry, don't cry)—doesn't mean my grandmother doesn't frighten me a little, especially when she's mad. "You ruined her proposal!"

"I found a way to help her—" Mirabel stammers.

I think of the way Isabela looked at Mariano.

Now that Mirabel mentions it, I'm not sure that's how you look at someone who's supposed to be part of your dreams.

"The candle burned brighter than I've ever seen—"

"Mirabel," Abuela snaps.

I glance up at Abuela's window. I'm not sure I would call the candle brighter. In fact, it doesn't look so good. I know just how it feels. Trying to shine its brightest and failing miserably.

"Abuela—"

"Because the candle has nothing to do with you!"

I can feel the pang in my sister's heart as if it were in my own. I know what it's like to want so desperately to make the family proud. Before I lost my gift, I knew that everyone would always be proud of my strength—I mean, sometimes they didn't seem to notice or bother to thank me, but they would still be proud of me. No one wants to hear that something as important as the Madrigal candle has nothing to do with them.

Mirabel speaks softly now. "I am in the vision for a reason. I'm supposed to help us." Her eyes meet Abuela's. "I can save the magic. You just have to hear—"

"You have to stop this, Mirabel," Abuela says, breaking their stare. Yikes, this is not good. As she speaks, a tremor shakes the courtyard's bricks. "The cracks," Abuela says, sweeping her arms to show all the damage done to the house already, "are here because of *you*. You were jealous of Antonio's gift and the cracks began."

Whoa. That's harsh. My heart skips a beat. I knew that our primito's gift day was hard on my little sister, but I don't know that I believe *this*. Mirabel's face is pale. "No!"

"Luisa lost her powers because you interfered!"

I sink back into the shadows. I don't want to make anything worse. I just want everyone to get along. I look down at my hands, my arms that used to be so strong. The only thing this body is good for now is gentle hugs. But I don't want to believe it's actually Mirabel's fault.

"That's not fair!"

"Isabela is confused because of you!" Abuela stomps her foot. Cracks fan out from under it. "Bruno left our family because of you! The candle is dying because of you, Mirabel!"

If I were Mirabel, I would have crumbled into a bucket of tears by now. But Mirabel stands strong. She doesn't seem to notice the cracking now. Her eyes are blank, sad. "He said this would happen. That you would only see the worst in me."

The candle in Abuela's window flickers, the flame burning up and then down, casting strange shadows on the walls that are still cracking. It seems like wherever the shadow lands, the walls crack more. I'm feeling a little uneasy under the balcony. Should we be, um, moving to safety? I wonder.

"You're wrong," Mirabel says quietly.

Even the cracking seems to quiet at that statement.

"Luisa will never be strong enough."

I knew it. I knew it was my fault. Why can't I be everywhere at once? Another crack shoots out from under Abuela's feet. I hear the unmistakable scrape of furniture—the dining room table— sliding across the tile floors beyond the courtyard. I should go see if I can help.

"Isabela isn't perfect enough. Bruno isn't good enough."

My mouth gapes open. Isabela doesn't look shocked to hear Mirabel say this. In fact, she looks almost pleased. Mirabel isn't just talking about me not being strong enough. Is it possible that maybe none of us is *enough*?

"And the night I didn't get my gift was the night you stopped believing in me!" Mirabel says. More cracks appear, some beneath my own feet. I watch them crawl up the walls, around the pillars.

The bricks rattle and shake. "The house is dying because no one in this family is good enough for you. That's why the magic is dying!"

In the distance, I hear voices. People from town seem to be gathering outside. I smell smoke, maybe from lanterns and torches. There's fear in the air. *It's okay. It's okay,* I repeat to myself, even though it's so obviously *not* okay. Another picture crashes to the floor. I run toward it, but then I hear another crash in the other direction and I run that way. *It's okay. It's okay.* The cracks are everywhere. I can't be everywhere at once! I'm light-headed, and my breathing is fast and shallow. I think I'm going to have a panic attack.

"You have no idea what I have done for this family!" Abuela cries.

Cracks in the floor make Mirabel unsteady. "You have no idea what you've done *to* this family!"

In Abuela's window, the candle is withering, nothing like its usual golden, glowing, magical self. There's almost nothing left of it. It flickers and oozes black, ashy soot. I've never seen anything so awful. I think I'm going to puke. This is *so* not okay.

Abuela stares at the fading candle. It feels like pain is all around us now instead of magic. There are shouts from outside and deep rumbles from within. Beams creak and groan. My instinct is to roll up my sleeves, readying myself to hoist, pull, lift, move anything that's needed. But then I remember how useless I am. Stupid!

More cracks appear, bigger ones, running between my grandmother and my sister. *It's not okay. It's not okay.* I'm pretty sure I'm crying now. Is that weak? If so, I don't care. I'd really like my mami right about now. Outside, the commotion and the cries of panicked voices are rising. It sounds like the whole town is right beyond our doors. I can't decide if I should check on that or stay here.

Abuela glares at Mirabel. "I have dedicated my life to protect our family, our home." Her voice is strong and firm but sad. So sad.

The floor under our feet begins to rock and sway. Casita is breaking.

"Open your eyes!" Mirabel says to Abuela. "Our family is falling apart because of *you!*"

Plaster crumbles and falls to the ground in dusty clouds. A chandelier tips and breaks. Everything is literally falling apart. New fissures rip at the house, nearly cracking it in two. I *know* that I'm needed now, but I'm powerless. If I had my strength, I would fix the wall. No, wait, the pillar. No, what about the staircase?

But I realize it's just not possible. No amount of strength can save Casita now. Horrible noises groan from the house as the walls tumble, the roof tiles break, the doors snap. A deep fissure splits the house. The crack snakes its way to the Madrigal candle, which is almost completely burned down. Its weak flame flickers.

Did I mention I'm afraid of the dark?

Chapter 19 * Mirabel

AROUND US, the family runs in panic as the Casita cracks and crumbles. The grand table in the dining room splinters, the balcony railing above us splinters. The cracks are all heading toward Abuela's room.

"The candle!" Tía Pepa cries. "Save the candle!"

Isabela swings into action. She tries to use her vines to reach the candle, but they die around her. All the flowers in the destroyed courtyard are black and withered. "No!" she cries as she looks up in time to see her beautiful door fizzle.

"Casita!" I yell. The house helps me climb toward the roof. Camilo is right behind me. But then I hear a sizzle, and when I look back, his door has gone out, just like Isabela's. "Ah, no!" It's terrible to see cheery, joking Camilo's stricken face.

"Pepa!" shouts Felix. "You have to stop the wind."

My tía is crying, but the wind keeps whipping us. "I can't!" She takes a deep breath, tries to concentrate. Then she looks around. "Where is Antonio?"

Dolores runs toward us, yelling, "What? What?" as if she can't hear anything.

"Where's Antonio?" Pepa asks. Dolores runs upstairs and drags Antonio away from his room. The tree inside crashes through the door just as the magic is snuffed out. Dolores and Antonio are hurled across the courtyard. The tapirs stampede and the macaws fly in frightened flocks.

"No!" shouts Pepa.

Felix catches Antonio in his arms. Dolores has landed safely in a wheelbarrow, thanks to some quick moves by Casita. That gives me an idea.

"Casita, you have to get everyone out!"

Luisa tries to lift beams and furniture, but she has no more strength than I do. The smiling family portraits—Pepa and Felix's wedding picture, the sepia photo of Abuela and Abuelo, the goofy shot of us cousins making faces at the camera—that line the walls all slip to the floor, their frames busted.

"¡Vamos!" Felix is leading his family out of the house.

One by one the doors of my family's rooms fade, their magic dying. Bruno's tower has disintegrated into piles of sand. I hope he's okay.

"Vámonos, todos," Papá says. Mamá takes one last look as her kitchen crumbles and the tiles shatter, the plates snap, the pots break in pieces. "Come on, come on."

I look up and see that the candle is still there

in Abuela's window. But it looks impossible to reach—especially without any magic. The house, which is barely a house at this point, is crumbling. I have to reach the candle. I use the balcony railing and get a foothold to reach the roof. Carefully, I walk along the roof, my feet clacking the tiles. One tile breaks away and crashes on the courtyard floor below.

"Mirabel, no!" Mamá cries.

I don't stop. I keep reaching, keep trying. I grab for the candle. Another tile slips; my feet go out from under me. I can feel Casita using its last breath to shield me. I don't let go of the candle, even as I tumble. The Casita spits debris and dust. It's gone. The house—the rooms, the courtyard, the tower, all gone. Nothing but a pile of rubble. And me.

"No wonder she didn't get a gift," someone says. I flinch as if someone had hit me. It hurts because I know it's true.

A toucan lands on a pile of bricks. Antonio clambers over the debris toward it, but the bird flies away.

The family is disappointed in me. Everyone knows it was my fault. Mirabel who has no gift. Abuela was right. I'm destroying the family. No, I've *destroyed* the family. Isabela was right. I ruin everything. I know what I have to do.

I stand up but trip on a broken bit of brick. My grandmother doesn't move, doesn't reach out to try to catch me. When I fall, my skirt snags. I yank it free and slink away. I slip out of what's left of the house.

"Where is Mirabel?" my mother asks. "Mirabel?"

I don't turn around. I know the family— everyone—is better off without me.

Soon I'm deep in the forest. My mind is numb. I just walk and walk. The trees remind me of Isabela's plants and Antonio's jungle. Herbs scent the air, making me think of Mamá and her cooking. A bird calls and I think of Papá's music. But I push thoughts of my family from my mind. They don't need me and my destruction. I didn't—couldn't— help them.

I trudge through the woods, not quite sure where I'm going. One foot in front of the other. I keep playing the last few moments over in my head. The vision, the visit to Isabela's room, the laughing with my sister, the candle, Abuela. Somehow things got worse and then better and then really worse. Each time I consider it, I know it was all my fault. It started with me. Abuela said it began when I was five. *Ever since you didn't get your gift.*

The mountains surrounding the Encanto—or what's left of it—are littered with rockslides. I pick my way through the boulders, wishing Luisa were here to move them out of my way. Except she doesn't have her gift anymore.

I climb over fallen branches and tree limbs.

The embroidery on my blouse snags. The threads on my skirt unravel, the images I had sewn fading just like the Madrigal family. I trip over and over, scraping both knees and one shin. I wish Mamá could cure the cuts. If I were Isabela, I wouldn't be so clumsy. I scramble between shrubs. My skirt catches again, and this time it tears. Ruined. Just like Isabela's proposal dinner.

As I make my way through the mountain pass, the one that had newly appeared, like a scar upon the land. A jagged crack that breaks the earth and the Encanto apart. Apparently, the depths of my destruction spread farther than even I thought. My heart sinks deeper. My eyes sink to the ground in despair.

When I hear the rushing of water over the pounding of my heart do I look up. A river appears, and I stop. I make my way to the bank. Sitting on the water's edge, I can see my own reflection. And then another figure appears in the mirror of the water.

"Mirabel." The voice of Abuela is quiet beside me.

"You were right," I say in a small voice. "You were right about me, and now our home is . . ."

My gaze moves upstream toward rapids that tumble over rocks, the mist hanging low over the water. A yellow leaf, like a little butterfly, floats down the river.

"Of all the places you could have gone, you found this place," Abuela says. "I never thought I could ever come back here. This river is where we were given our miracle."

The water sings over the river rocks and the breeze whistles through the trees. The silence between us feels like something as strong as magic.

"Where Abuelo Pedro . . ."

Abuela nods. "It was a different life."

I wish I had thought to ask about her story and try to understand where she came from—her side. To be curious about my grandfather. But it always felt like something you don't talk about. So many things we don't talk about. Like Bruno. My eyes sting, and I take off my glasses and wipe them on my blouse.

"You're like him. I never was." Abuela gazes out over the river. "I remember when I first met him. Love at first sight. Silly, isn't it?" Abuela laughs—a sad laugh. But I don't think it's silly at all. If I squint, I can see in her the young bride she once was in the old photo that hangs—well, used to hang—in the Casa. "We were so young and in love. So hopeful. When we got married, I was the happiest I had ever been before—the happiest I've ever been since. Our wedding was the best day of my life. I saved our wedding candle because I wanted to remember that day."

Candle? I want to ask Abuela if the Madrigal candle is the same as her wedding candle, but I see that she is deep in thought, lost in memories.

"He was thrilled when we found out I was having triplets. I was overwhelmed at the thought, but Pedrito was certain of our happiness." Abuela smiles, but then her eyes darken. "It would have been perfect. It could have been perfect. But then the city became dangerous. It was no place to raise a family. Especially not three babies. Pedro was brave and smart, and he knew we had to leave."

Abuela tells me about how they traveled into the wilderness with only their candle to guide them. They weren't the only family leaving, trying to escape violence and unrest, searching for a better life. But danger seemed to follow them, and their group of fellow travelers became trapped by bandits between the river and the mountains. Here. In this very spot. Where we sit on the riverbank. No wonder she's sad. Abuela tells me how Pedro kissed each of the babies—the babies who grew up to be Mamá and Pepa and Bruno.

"He kissed me," Abuela says, her voice that of a young woman. Her eyes are closed as she tells me that he assured me everything was going to be okay. Then he went back and tried to talk to the bandits, to reason with them. But they were villains. He died and never returned. And all she could do was pray.

"Then they came for me. For us." I gently embrace my grandmother as she sighs with the memories. I think of the last time we sat this close: my gift day, the day I disappointed her. Now she looks at me, tears in her eyes but a sad smile on her face. "But then I put my hand to the earth, and the candle—the candle burned so brightly. It flooded the ravine with a golden glow. Oh, Mirabel, if you had seen it. The bandits were pushed back by the light, almost as if it were a wall, a wave, a curtain. The mountains grew as if the earth itself were protecting me. Us."

"That became the Encanto?"

"Sí," she says. "I knew I was lucky. We were lucky, me and my babies. Blessed. And I needed to make Pedro proud, to make his sacrifice worth it. Our family took care of the village, took care of one another. Until . . ."

My body tenses. I want her to stop talking.

I know the "until" is when I didn't get my gift. I nod sadly, feeling the familiar weight of the entire Madrigal family on my tired shoulders.

"It didn't start with the day you didn't get your gift. It started before then. When Bruno and I argued, and he disappeared. When Isabela could never be quite perfect enough for me. When Luisa was never working quite hard enough. And now . . ."

Abuela opens the locket that hangs from her chatelaine. Abuelo Pedro.

"For so long, I've been hoping that if I made our family strong enough," Abuela says, "if we worked hard enough, his sacrifice would matter."

I lean against her shoulder and peer at the photo. Pedro is young and smiling. He looks proud and eager for life. I can see a little of Mamá in the way his eyes sparkle. His fine nose reminds me of Luisa's strong face. His hair—well, it's tamed by pomade, but I recognize the texture from my own. I find myself smiling at his picture.

"But if he could see me now, he would be so disappointed in me."

My head snaps up to stare at my grandmother. *He* would be disappointed in *her*?

"You were right," she continues. "You did not break our family, Mirabel. I did."

Neither of us moves.

I'm stunned. The weight seems to lift from my shoulders. I sit up straighter, taller.

Abuela broke our family? It doesn't seem possible. She might be little, but she's stronger than Luisa in many ways. She might be old and wrinkled, but she can be more perfect than Isabela. She might be impatient sometimes, but she doesn't need food to heal us like Mamá. My abuela has all the gifts.

I look out over the river, at the forest, the sky. I see a flutter. A single butterfly, its wings iridescent blue, lands on a twig in the middle of the river.

"When I was little," I say to Abuela, taking her hands in mine, "you told me a story about miracles. About how even in our darkest moments, there's light." Realizing what I need to do, I help her to her feet and lead her to the water. "Hope, where you least expect it."

If this is where Pedro was last with her, maybe she needs to remember. Remember in a different way. See it in a different light.

"You carried so much, all alone, for so long." I slosh into the water. She follows me like she's the little girl. "Abuelo would be so proud. Because he would see what I do."

We're in the water now. The butterfly slowly opens and closes its wings in rhythm with the river's forward movement.

"You love your family. You held the candle. You prayed to the earth." As I say these words, I can see the picture Abuela painted. What happened here was sad but also beautiful. Everything can be two things at once if you look at it the right way. Not *either, or*. But *and*. The Encanto glistens with magic and also holds real life. Magic *and* reality.

"We were given this miracle because of *you*, Abuela."

"I . . ." my grandmother begins. "I asked Pedro for help." She gazes at me as if she's seeing me—really seeing me—for the first time. "And you were here all along." She reaches out and touches my face, just like she did on the morning of my gift day. "Mi vida, you *are* the miracle."

The clouds break apart then. We're bathed in bright sunlight. The light over the river dances in pinks and golds. Abuela releases my hand, standing straighter and taller. A shaft of sunlight shines on the butterfly, and it flits away. But it doesn't go far. Soon it's joined by a second butterfly, both sets of wings dancing in the sun. I point them out to Abuela. Then several more butterflies swoop down from the treetops. Now there are dozens—no, hundreds—of other butterflies. An arc of golden flashing wings builds and surrounds us. I can feel the magic all around us. Abuela grips my hand.

Her fingers curl around mine, protecting and reassuring me. Thousands of wings blend with the golden sunlight, bathing the river, the forest, and us in a warm pink glow.

And then, up ahead, we see a dark shape. A figure crashes into the river, spraying water everywhere. I hear a whinny. It's a horse. And on the horse is a rider—sort of. Tío Bruno is seated awkwardly on the poor pony, listing to one side.

"She didn't do this!" he shouts, splashing us with water as he nears us. "I gave her a vision! I told her, I was like . . ." Bruno tumbles off the horse as Abuela stares at him. "And she's—she's, like, a good person. She only wanted to help." Bruno trips on his own feet. "I don't care what you think of me, but if you're too stubborn to see—"

"Brunito," Abuela says. She reaches out her arms and he shrinks back. But then she folds him in a hug.

He looks over her shoulder at me. "I feel like I missed something important."

I laugh. "Come on!" I grab the horse's reins and help Abuela up.

"Uh," Bruno says. "What's happening? Where are we going?"

I climb on Bruno's horse, turning the animal around. "Home," I say and let the butterflies lead us through the Encanto.

Chapter 20 * Isabela

OF ALL THE STRANGE THINGS that have happened today—creating beautifully ugly plants with Mirabel and the candle going out and Casita crumbling—perhaps the strangest one of all is happening right now. Down the path from the mountain comes a horse—a sad, sort of homely horse—with the three least likely people: Abuela, Mirabel, and Bruno. The three of them are led by a ribbon of butterflies, like a huge bouquet of flowers.

Pepa is coming toward me with Antonio riding on her shoulders. He points to the sky as he spots the butterflies. We laugh at the surprise, the beauty. Camilo and Felix come running from the ruined house with Luisa. They, too, look up and gape as they watch the butterflies. And their mouths hang open even wider when they spot Mirabel on the horse, riding like the wind, with Abuela clinging to her and Bruno riding awkwardly behind.

Our smiles from the sight of the butterflies fade as we realize that the three of them riding so fast—together—must mean that something is terribly wrong. Is Abuela hurt? Sick? But as they get closer, I see that they're both . . . smiling. And so is Bruno. I don't see anything to smile about.

From behind me, I hear voices. People from town are streaming toward the Casa, shouting and calling, wanting to know what happened. My heart aches for them. The Familia Madrigal is supposed to take care of and support these people. I look around. Casita is in shambles, just a pile of rubble and broken tiles. From our perch in the Encanto, we can see that the village is a pile of debris, too. Many houses are damaged; a few donkeys roam free. The plaza is cracked and littered with trash. Now what? I realize that I have no idea what to do. Before, I always knew that flowers could make things better, make Abuela proud, make the family proud. But I know that a few flowers won't fix the house. Or the Encanto.

For a moment, when Mirabel sees the demolished Casa, her smile falters. But then she helps Abuela down from the horse and her grin returns.

The crowd approaches the house, and then they slow and stop. One by one, each person notices the butterflies. Then they see Mirabel and Abuela.

"Mirabel," I hear Mamá say. She and Papá look tired and worried as they rush to hug Mirabel and

Abuela. Even though I'm heartbroken about the state of the magic and the Casa, I'm so glad to see my family together. I step closer.

"Where did you go?" Mamá asks, her eyes dark.

"Mamá," Mirabel says, her face shining. "We're going to be okay."

Luisa, coming toward our family, too, steps forward. "Mira, the magic is gone." She tries to lift the homely horse to demonstrate.

Mirabel smiles. It's the same smile she gave me when she was little. The day before her gift day, she came running into my room, so excited and full of expectation. And she kept smiling, even after she didn't get her gift. Mirabel always brought people together, lifted them up. Her eyes twinkle behind her glasses and I find myself wondering what the world looks like to her. She clearly sees the best in others, seeing the possibilities. Sometimes the things that we can't see ourselves.

"There's another way." She's the only one smiling as she looks at the house and the family. I try to focus on her, ignore the devastation of our beloved Casita. "I thought that everything had to be one way. I thought I knew everything about each of us. But I realized . . ."

We all move closer. My parents and my sister. My aunt and uncles and cousins. Even Bruno and Abuela. The family, together. It's like the best kind of magic. The Madrigals form a circle around Mirabel.

"I realized that if you look closely, you'll see something different than you thought you saw. I mean, we all struggle, right? A lot more than we let other people know."

I shift uncomfortably from one foot to the other. I think about how tired I am of making everything beautiful and being perfect all the time. Mirabel saw me cast off the perfect ways and try something that felt more me. Is it possible, I wonder, that others feel like that, too?

"I know what you mean, Mirabel," I whisper. Then, louder, I say, "I don't always want to have the perfect dress, the perfect hair. Sometimes I might want to be something else, something more, you know?"

Mirabel rushes toward me and grabs me in a huge hug. At first, I want to back up and push her away like I always do. But then I think about what she said, that maybe everyone struggles. Maybe Mirabel needs a hug as much as I do. I squeeze her back and we laugh. "Your ugly-beautiful plants were awesome, Isabela!" she says. "We need more of that in our lives."

"You mean, like," Luisa says, "like, maybe there's other things I could do for the family? Things that maybe don't require these?" She holds up her arm and flexes her muscle.

"Well, we still might need those sometimes," Mirabel says, going in for a hug in Luisa's strong arms.

Luisa nods. "Sometimes our gifts can feel a little like a burden. Even when, you know, burdens are your specialty."

"Exactly!" Mirabel says. "Sometimes change is good."

"I'm kind of the expert at change," Camilo pipes up. "Change isn't so bad. Maybe I could change in other ways, too. Like, maybe I can be myself?"

"Oh, Camilo," Dolores says, and squeezes him. "I know you can be more than other people. And not just because I can hear so well." I study my cousin Dolores, thinking about what it would be like to hear *everything*. Maybe she'd like a break from her gift, too. "Sometimes," she says, "maybe, I'd like to speak, too? Not just listen."

Pepa smiles at Dolores. "We'd like that," she says. "Ay, ay, ay," she cries. "I might start crying."

"No!" Felix shouts. "Then we'll drown!" He laughs and grabs his wife in a tight embrace. They kiss in front of everyone. Camilo groans, but I smile and clap. I hope that someday I can find the person of my dreams and we'll love each other like Pepa and Felix do.

"It's okay," says Mirabel. "Tía Pepa can be

herself. She can cry if she wants. Everyone should be who they want to be."

"I should have talked about Bruno," Abuela says. She reaches out and squeezes her son's hand. Bruno hides inside his poncho, but we can all see the embarrassed grin on his face.

"I wanted to cry when Bruno left," Pepa says, sniffling.

Abuela approaches Pepa and takes her hand. "I wish I had known that, hija."

"Look!" Antonio cries. With one hand he clutches a stuffed jaguar and with the other he points at what's left of the walls. But instead of destruction, the cracks are slowly receding, like the opposite of a vine growing.

"I guess maybe I don't want to be so perfect all the time," I say softly. Abuela looks at me with surprise. "I mean, I still love flowers"—I glance at Mirabel—"I'd like to find out what else I can do."

"Maybe you want to learn to play the piano?"

Papá says. He holds up a broken piano string. "Or maybe we'll learn how to build one?"

"Who wants to learn to cook?" Mamá says. She holds a basket of arepas that escaped the destruction of the kitchen. Camilo grabs one in each hand. Antonio tries to feed one to his little stuffed animal.

"Oh, you guys!" says Mirabel. "I think it's hug time!"

Chapter 21 * Mirabel

MAYBE IT SOUNDS DUMB, but my heart hurts with joy. The house may be in shambles, but the family is intact—better than before, because now we have Bruno back with us. Amid all the hugging everyone's doing, I look over at my uncle. He gives me a shy thumbs-up. I grin and return it. The weirdos of the family have to stick together.

"I'm sorry about the Casa, Abuela," I say as the hugfest continues around us.

"Mija, it's not your fault." She looks around at the house and the family. The townspeople are coming in for hugs, too. "And the house? Well, if we can fix our family, we can surely fix a house, can't we?"

"We can?"

And that's when I realize that the people from the town aren't just here for the hug-o-rama. They're carrying tools—shovels and trowels and buckets. And so begins the biggest home remodeling project ever. The donkey delivery guy fetches materials from town. Señor Rendon's donkeys carry loads of canvas and wood. Señora Ruiz and Señora Uriarte hand out cups of hot café con leche to everyone.

All the Madrigals help, working together, which is pretty amazing. Isabela scrubs the floor of the foyer, and her dress turns black with grime. Luisa asks for help when she gets tired. As soon as the kitchen is functioning, Mamá makes piles of arepas, which Papá delivers to anyone who wants one. Camilo lifts Antonio so he can hang the pictures. Dolores is happy to do any chore, but she talks *so* much, the only person who wants to work beside her is Mariano—who can't seem to take his eyes off her! Abuela oversees everything, taking a rest when she needs it. Piece by piece, each brick, each tile, each carpet is replaced. And as our home is rebuilt, it becomes stronger than ever.

It takes both more time and less time than I would have imagined to repair our home. For three days, everyone in the Encanto works, but eventually the Casa looks nearly like its old self again. The plaster is mostly smooth on the solid walls, and the family photos are hung—if a little crookedly. The courtyard bricks are even, and the ornate balcony railings are sturdy. Each terracotta roof tile is laid in place, ready to shelter us from any kind of weather the skies brings us.

And while everyone pitches in, Bruno works on his vision.

"What is it?" I ask, leaning over his shoulder. He's almost done—just a few more pieces to go.

"Patience, Mirabel," he grumbles. He can still be a little touchy.

I hug him around his neck. Bruno shrugs me off, but he's smiling. He can't help it. He's so glad to be part of the family again. "Don't be so grumpy, Tío!" I say as he slips in the last shard.

This is it. The final piece. I don't know if we need to see the future, to have Bruno tell us his vision. We can already see what's right in front of us: the Familia Madrigal working together and letting each person be true to themselves. I close my eyes.

"Open your eyes," Bruno says. "Tell us what you see."

Bruno's vision? It's the same. His vision came true: the house is fixed, and in front of it, in front of the cracked and formerly broken Casita, is me.

Bruno's vision hadn't been about me *breaking* the Casa, it had been about me *fixing* it!

I feel a presence beside me. Abuela.

"Mirabel, for you." Abuela pulls something from her pocket. She places something hard and round in my hands.

I look down. It's a doorknob. Just a plain doorknob, round and shiny. I'm confused until I glance at the house. With all this hard work, we've managed to complete the remodel—err, rebuild. Everything is in place . . . except the front door is missing its knob.

The family gathers around, the people from town behind them. I walk toward the house, clutching the doorknob. I hold it out and see a face reflected on its shiny surface. Me. It's me. I might not have fancy powers like my sisters, but I'm still me. I'm here.

"I'm here," I say. "Estoy aquí." To the house, to my family, to the world. "I am here."

And I slip the doorknob in place.

I stumble back as the door makes a whooshing sound. The ground beneath my feet seems to rock. The house trembles. Is it going to collapse? I've done it again! Ruined everything! But instead of collapsing, the house seems to take a deep breath, its walls expanding. The Madrigal candle reshapes itself and ignites. And suddenly, surrounding all of it is an explosion of butterflies brighter and bigger than the fireworks on Antonio's gift day. Butter-flies appear out of every crevice and cranny. The leaves in the trees become butterflies; the clouds in the sky take the shape of butterflies. The blue wings glitter, leaving waves of gold in their wake. They circle the house, reaching toward the sky and then back down again. A rainbow forms over Pepa's head. Luisa laughs and lifts both our parents high in the air. Isabela twirls and the bougainvil-lea twines its way up Bruno's tower—along with a couple of odd spiny cacti. And I am in the middle of it all. The butterflies swoop and glide. Magic swirls with them, embracing the family, the townspeople, the entire Encanto.

My Casa smiles at me and then pulls me in for a hug. I giggle. "Hello, Casita."

Epilogue

ONCE UPON A TIME, there was a family. Aunts and uncles, mothers and fathers, cousins and sisters, brothers . . . and one grandmother. Each member of the family was important and special. With their own kind of magic. It might have been hard to see. It might have looked different in some. But it was always there.

The family lived in a magical and wonderful

house in a beautiful encanto. Inside the house, there was a room for each person, a room as extraordinary and unique as him or her. My cousin Antonio had a jungle room where he bunked with all the animals. My sister Isabela had a garden room with flowers—and a few cacti. My other sister Luisa's room was just right for someone who's strong on the outside and pretty much a softie on the inside. Abuela had a room that honored her Pedro.

When people meet our family and see our Casita, they want to know where my family's magic comes from. And I always say it comes from the same place theirs does. It might be hard to see. It might look different than some. But it's always there.

"Can I take the blindfold off?" I ask.

"Not yet!" Bruno says as he helps me up the stairs to the balcony.

The magic might be in the person you'd least expect.

I can tell without looking that we're walking

past the doors to all the rooms. Their magic has returned, but all the doors look a little different than they used to. Bruno's door is no longer covered in cobwebs; Luisa's door doesn't reflect only her strength but her whole self. Isabela's door is more than just pretty flowers; she's a lot more complicated than that. My feet shuffle over the carpet. I know we're nearly at my own door. What used to be the nursery.

"Okay, you can look now!" Antonio shouts. He's jumping up and down with excitement.

It takes a moment for my eyes to adjust. Sometimes you just have to open your eyes. I wipe my glasses on my blouse just to be sure I'm seeing clearly.

The door that was so plain and ordinary is now magnificent. Isabela's flowers outline the frame. Luisa has added bright, strong colors. Antonio's animals are represented. There's a rainbow that could only be from Pepa. I see a little theater, perfect for performing rats . . . thanks to Tío Bruno.

I open the new door, and my room is more beautiful and fantastical than I ever could have imagined. You would never know that it used to be a plain nursery. A vine grows above the bed like a canopy. A chigüiro is curled up on my pillow like a stuffed animal. A heavy bookshelf is loaded with books. A cup of hot chocolate and a plate of arepas steams on the table. Everyone in my family has added a little something to my room.

"I love it!" I cry. I swipe away pesky tears. "You guys, I can't believe you did this. For me." I open my arms wide. "Hug time!"

"Vengan," Abuela says. "Come." But instead of hugging everyone as they stream into my new and improved room, she announces, "It's time for a family picture."

Everyone crowds in—Pepa and Felix, Papá and Mamá, Bruno and his rats, Antonio and his animals with Camilo and Dolores, my sisters, and Abuela. We smash together and make faces, smiling and laughing. We all shout, "La Familia Madrigal!"

Even though the flashbulb blinds me for a moment, I know I'm surrounded by people I love who love me, just the way I am.

The End